# KELLoRY
## THE WARLoCK

# KELLoRY
## THE WARLoCK

### LIN CARTER

**WILDSIDE PRESS**

*To four lovely ladies who write fantasy superbly: to C.J. Cherryh, Tanith Lee, Grail Undwin, and in particular, to Pat McIntosh, who is fond of Kellory.*

Published by Wildside Press LLC
www.wildsidepress.com

*Zao, Olymbris, Thoorana, Zephrondus, and Great Gulzund;*
*These five worlds circle the star Kylix in the Unicorn.*
*Now it is of Zephrondus that I would speak.*
*No eye but mine has looked upon her many-colored moons,*
*Her feather-trees, her vast and endless plains,*
*But I have voyaged thither in my dreams,*
*And from that far voyaging I bring this tale to you...*

—Song of Worlds,
from *The Chronicles of Kylix*, The First Book.

# PART 1

## DARK PALACE OF THE FLAME

# CHAPTER 1

## ON FIRE MOUNTAIN

It was the hour of sunfall. In the depths of the great green sea to the west, the sun-star, Kylix, died in a welter of crimson flame. And in the east the first of the three moons of Zephrondus had new-risen above the dark drear edges of the world, Sligon was its name: the Moon of Pallid Opal.

For three days now, the boy Kellory had made his slow and laborious way along the skyline of the mountains, and now he was in view of his goal at last. He stood on the scarps of glassy obsidian and stared upon Fire Mountain. And despite himself, he felt the taste of fear like brass upon his tongue.

He was tall, this youth, and nearly naked save for a scrap of cloth about his loins and dragonhide sandals strapped high on his long bare legs. Sun and wind had burnt him the hue of old, seasoned leather and his wild unruly mane of black hair—not yet woven in the single braid of a warrior—was held back from his eyes by a leathern thong about the brows. For all the bitter cold of the mountains and the fierce winds that, howling, roved about their wintry peaks, he went bare. The better to climb, unencumbered with the weight of furs: and, as well, he had dwelt among these icy peaks for five of his fifteen years, and the cold he was well accustomed to endure.

As the boy stared up at the great mountain, Yothlymbris, he felt aware again of the grim futility of his quest; yet the thought of turning back did not even occur to him. For five years had he fended for himself in this wild and lonely land, tracking the great apes of the mountains for his meat and, in winter, battling the snow wolves with flaming brands.

He had not seen or spoken to a human being now for three years. His life he held at little worth; what if he lose it among the perils of the peak? No one in all this world of Zephrondus would know or care of his passing, why then should he?

He was dark and lean, this boy, with hard, tough sinewy limbs and strength far beyond his young years. Under the wild mat of his unshorn mane, a narrow white scar snaked across his forehead to lose itself in his scowling black brows. Under those brows—strange in his dark, somber, bitter face—his eyes burned like weird green jewels. There was no laughter in them at all, nor softness in the hard, grim straight line of his mouth or the firm stubborn set of his well-molded jaw.

A long spear of *thoyak* wood was strapped across his broad shoulders. A crude dagger of rough-hammered iron lay in a scabbard strapped to his lean thigh. The cloth about his loins was held by a girdle of black supple leather about his waist, and fastened to this was a huge moontree-seed hollowed to make a water-gourd, and a coil of rope and a three-pronged bronze hook wherewith he had ascended the dizzying heights of the sheer cliff-walled chasms of these mountains. Save for these, he had nothing in the world. Except his memories, which burned like frozen iron. And the black leather glove he wore on his right hand.

Above him soared the sky-tall height of Yothlymbris: Fire Mountain, his people called it once. Now he saw the reason why. And, for the first time, he felt the sour taste of hopelessness.

Kellory was a savage of Barbaria, although his ancestors had been mighty kings. He could not read, neither could he write. And he had never seen a book in all his young life. Thus he had never heard the word *volcano*. But now as he stared up grimly at the flickering sheet of crimson flame that danced about the crest of Mount Yothlymbris, he knew why no man had ever come to the gates of Phazdaliom the Enchanter. With a moat of liquid fire about the castle on the crest, it was not surprising.

Not that any idle traveler would care to disturb the Green Enchanter, even without his blazing moat. In Zephrondus, as in every other world whereof I have knowledge (and they are legion), one does not lightly intrude upon the seclusion of magicians.

But Kellory had a very good reason: *vengeance!*

Now that he had paused long enough to catch his breath, he continued on his journey. From the glassy scarp whereon he stood, the chasm plunged down two thousand feet to dim enshadowed depths below. But across the chasm a flat boulder of black gneiss lay. If he could spring across the gap, he would be on the walls of Fire Mountain.

There was no spire or ledge above the level coign of gneiss which he could snag with the tri-pronged brazen hook that swung at his hip. So he would have to jump the gap. It was, or looked to be, twelve feet wide. So near. So very near. Yet to miss… He would not even live to feel the crimson agony as his body broke on the cruel rocks far below: the speed of his fall would smother him long ere he reached the bottom.

Kellory drew back to the farthest corner of the scarp of sleek obsidian—back, until his naked shoulders pressed against the ragged granite wall down which he had lithely clambered a few moments before. Then, bracing the sole of one foot against the wall, he pushed against it for extra leverage—and threw himself out, over the dizzying abyss and into space.

For one brief, flashing instant, he flew between earth and heaven. Then, in the next, he crashed flat, chest and arms and lean belly, against the edge of the black gneiss boulder. His legs hung over the lip of the chasm. His hands clawed desperately for a purchase on the smooth stone. They slipped, and he slid back a pace, so that his narrow hips were over the edge. But he bit his lip fiercely, and clawed for a purchase on the stone—and found one.

Slowly, inch by inch, he hauled himself up over the edge until he could slide one bare knee over the ledge.

At length, he lay flat on the gneiss boulder, exhausted, sobbing for breath, aching in every muscle, bruised.

But he had traversed the chasm. And he was on Fire Mountain at last.

# CHAPTER 2

## THE BURNING BRIDGE

It took him most of the night to scale the rugged sides of Mount Yo-thlymbris. Kellory was as agile as a monkey: every inch sinewy muscle. He had a fearless head for heights, and a recklessness that amounted to daredeviltry. But his right hand, gloved in black leather, was stiff and useless, and lack of it greatly hampered his ability to climb.

From scarp to scarp he went, while the Opal Moon rode up the zenith; from spire to spire and ledge to ledge he labored, while the Emerald Moon and the Moon of Amber climbed to join their sister on the heights. Dawn was a pallid ghost haunting the world's far eastern rim when he came to the crest at last.

And gazed upon the Lake of Flame.

It was a glimpse into the Inferno, that lake. Red light beat up from it, and poisonous winds like the breath of the desert simoon blew over those burning waves. The bitter stench of sulphur hung heavy on the air. Kellory crawled to the edge of the lava lake and peered over, though the baking heat made his fierce green eyes ache and water.

Imagine a restless mirror of sullen, glowing crimson. A yellow froth of sulphurous foam bescummed the sluggish waves of the liquid flame. Little serpents of bright canary fire flickered and crawled over the wrinkled, cherry-red surface of the lava. The light that glowed up from it was like the breath of a furnace. Such a deathly, incandescent lake smolders before the brass gates of Pandemonium, city of hell.

Kellory could not survive the Luciferian embrace of those thick, crawling waves for an instant. Like a moth in a candle-flame he would crisp and char. But cross it he must.

He circled the lake of fiery brimstone. The margin was like no other land on all Zephrondus. The up-spewings of the blazing moat, the stony vomitings, lay curdled and scaly like petrified black serpents, in a Lao-coön-tangle of porous, glass-sharp lava-stone. Aye, had it not been for the tough sandals of dragonhide he wore on his feet, high-laced over the ankles, the sharp-bladed stony serpents would probably have slashed his feet to gory ribbons, as if he had walked barefoot across a field of naked razors.

But then, few men ever came to this place, for few indeed were they who would trouble the seclusion of the Green Enchanter…

Amidst the lake of liquid fire, a black spire lifted. The crest of that spire was hewn (by, it was whispered, no human hand, but through the uncanny artifice of captive djinn) into a fantastic black castle. Through the drifting fumes of powdery yellow sulphur, he could see the looming bulk: an ebon mass of walls, turrets, pylons, domes, columns. Glass-smooth they were, and the changeful and wavering red fight of the lava moat was eerily reflected therein, as in warped and ebon mirrors.

In that weird black castle, carven from the mountain peak, dwelt Phazdaliom the Green Enchanter. And Kellory would gain his gates or perish.

And then he saw the bridge.

All of harsh red iron it was, spanning the fiery lake like a Titan's scimitar. The boy's heart sank within him. He had hoped to gain entry into the Enchanter's dark palace by secret and devious paths; but this looked the only means. It was walk the bridge, or swim the moat—and flesh cannot endure the burning kiss of those red waves.

Like a gliding shadow he crept to the portal of the bridge. Here iron pillars loomed, and they were worked to the leering likeness of devil-heads, with mirrored balls of black glass for eyes, wherein whose orbs the red fires of the lake blazed and crawled with sentient movements.

Eyes of slithering fire stared down at the boy who stood before the gate. Dagger-fanged jaws of rust-enscaled iron gaped in cruel mockery. And upon the brows of those snarling masks was cut the Sign of Fear.

But Kellory must go forward now. So, defiantly, he set one sandaled foot upon that bridge—

And sprang back with a gasp of pain! Crouching, he peered at the sole of his leathern sandal. It was black and smoking as if a burning brand had been pressed against it but a moment before. And again his spirits sank within him: of course! After numberless aeons through which the iron bridge had arched above those incandescent waves, the metal had soaked up the furnace-hearted heat.

The iron bridge was red-hot, and it burned like fire. He could not go ten steps before his sandals would crisp and sear. To go farther would mean he must crawl between the wizard's gates, with feet mere blackened knobs of charred and useless flesh!

# CHAPTER 3

## THE AVENUE OF AUTOMATONS

Kellory fell to his knees before the frowning portcullis of the Enchanter's castle, panting for breath, stifling in the sulphurous air of the moat, eyes streaming.

He had traversed the burning bridge by a simple expedient. Thoroughly soaking his leathern sandals in water from the moontree gourd that hung at his waist, he had dared the arch of glowing steel. The boy could run like a deer: many tunes his fleetness of foot had saved him from capture by a Thungoda war party man-hunting in the mountains; now his flying feet had carried him safely across the span of red-hot iron. But his sandals, dried in the baking heat, were charred and smoldering. He tore them from his blistered feet with shaking fingers, and hurled them into the flaming moat, together with the spear strapped to his shoulders, which encumbered his movements. Gingerly favoring his raw and tender feet, he climbed erect and looked about him. He stood before the palace gate…and it stood open, a titanic valve of ancient black wood that must have weighed a ton. The Sigil of Phazdaliom was worked on the front of this enormous door: an open, unsleeping Eye picked out in glittering dust of emeralds.

He glided silently within the open port and crept into the inky shadows of a great pillar.

Without, all had been baking heat and sulphurous smoke. But the moment he crossed the threshold of the dark palace, it was as if an invisible barricade held back the beating flames of the lava moat. For here within, the air was fresh and clean and dewy. Bruised, aching, running with oily perspiration and smeared from crown to heel with ashes and dirt, the tired boy leaned against the cool stone of the column, drinking in the pure sweet air thankfully.

But there was no time to rest. The intolerable thirst for vengeance had driven him this far—where no man else of all the world below had ever dared to come—and it would be an irony of ironies, should the unseen hand of the Enchanter strike him down before he had pierced the inner heart of the citadel. So he went forward on hesitant feet, green eyes burning like some jungle beast's as they searched the night-black shadows, alert for a trap, wary for the slightest motion, sound, or sign of peril.

He traversed a column-lined arcade and found himself at the mouth of a long avenue lined with statues. Beyond, at the end of this way, rose the inner castle, a gloomy mass against the pearly curtain of dawn: a fantastic thronging of minarets, arcades, towers and turrets, that lifted tier by tier into the clear morning. He saw that the castle was a mass of brooding blackness—save for one ominous window, tall and narrow and pointed, that burned with green light like an unsleeping eye; like the emerald Eye emblazoned on the wizard's door. It gazed down at him, a blank, cold glaze of icy phosphorescence, like the vigilant orb of some colossal ebon-mailed dragon, coiled about a secret treasure. A chill went through him as he looked at that one ominous window, blazing with light while all the castle else went slumbering and dark. But he went on.

The avenue, he perceived by the nacreous morning light, was strewn with crushed diamonds. They caught the morning in a tangle of dazzling rays, like the wink and glitter of some enormous ice field that shimmered and sparkled under the slow uncoiling fires of the aurora. Strange it was to tread that incredible pave, strewn—almost contemptuously—with the wealth of a thousand Emperors. But he went down the avenue of statues with a lightsome tread, one hand on the hilt of his dagger, eyes roaming warily the thick-mantled shadows that lay beyond. And ever and anon his gaze lifted to meet again the cold phosphorescent scrutiny of that window that burned like a dragon's open eye.

*And then he froze with incredulous horror.*

For the statues…moved!

He had thought them mere idols of hewn and carven stone, but now he saw they were fashioned each from shining steel. Like fantastic suits of goblin armor they stood in their ranked scores, lining the glittering avenue of diamonds. But, if armor, not…untenanted. For steel arms raised, stiffly brandishing fantastic pikes and scimitars of burnished steel, and, behind the frozen leer of mask-like visors, eyes of sentient crystal flashed with yellow topaz fire. Weirdly crested helms turned creakingly to face the dawn, and claw-like metal hands lifted mace and brand and morning star with jerking, mechanical movement.

A thrill of unbelief went through the shrinking boy. But he remembered, then: the old shaman of his tribe, that once had been a high priest of the gods in the greatness of the Lost Kingdom, had told him in whispers of these creatures. *The automatons of the Enchanter—the living warriors of soulless steel!* How could he have forgotten the terrible and undying guardians of the dark palace?

But—oddly—they seemed to see him not. The crystalline gaze that burned mindlessly behind the mask-like visors was lifted only to the morn. A wave of relief went through him, and he crept on down the avenue of shattered diamonds as the mechanical automatons of Phazdaliom made their salute to the new-born day.

# CHAPTER 4

## THE CORRIDOR OF BLOOD

Here, too, in the inmost citadel, the portals stood open as if in silent invitation to the trespasser. Silent as a gliding shadow or a drifting ghost, the bare brown figure of the boy crept through the marble doorway, which was carven in the likeness of befanged and yawning serpent-jaws, and vanished into the gloom that lay beyond.

He paused in the dense shadows to take stock of his surroundings. And, as his eye flitted from here to there, a vast awe awoke within his savage young heart—and a cold, creeping dread, as well.

He stood at the edge of a colossal rotunda. The pave was all of snowy marble veined and laced with frozen veils of pallid rose. Around the circular wall of this rotunda, which was fitted with plates of brass that flashed like shining gold, rose slender and serpentine pilasters of lucent alabaster. Up and up the graceful spiraling pillars went, to support a vast dome of milky glass that flushed rich crimson with the fires of dawn.

It was not the purity of the rare stone that filled the lad with awe and dread, but the shocking and disquieting knowledge that this vast space was *too huge*. It must have been half a mile from one side to the other… and that was far too enormous for the size of the citadel. A weird thrill went through him, and he felt the touch of nameless and cosmic fear like a cold wind blowing on his neck from invisible gulfs.

*The interior of the citadel was larger than the exterior!* Icy globules of sweat burst out on his brow and on his naked breast. This seeming contravention of the very laws of the physical universe was, somehow, more disquieting than all the ghouls and monstrous mantichores with which his imagination had peopled the palace of the Enchanter. It was as if, here within the wizard's house, space itself was twisted awry and subtly bent to new dimensions.

Somehow, he did not dare cross that vast mesa of snowy marble to its distant farther side. Instead he crept around the enormous floor, keeping well within the shadow cast by the pillars.

He came to a doorway hung with night-dark purples, and crept there-through.

He found himself in a curious antechamber, the walls whereof were hung with a weird tapestry of woven sword-blades that swayed and swung with faint, clashing, silvery music to the breath of winds unfelt by him. The antechamber was carpeted with the skins of hippogriff and chimera.

Like a brown shadow he crossed the strange chamber where the arras of interlaced and razory steel slithered and sang to the touch of unknown winds, and came to a curious doorway.

It was an arch, a continuous curve, made of yellowed ivory, and the ivory was *all of one piece.* Seventeen feet high the ivory arch soared, and nine feet from side to side it was: the boy's imagination shuddered away from attempting to conceive the vast enormity of the Beast from whose *single tusk* so incredible an archway had been cut.

The ivory arch was hung with a curious curtain of gold tissue. Thin and pallid and transparent as vapor was this delicate silken hanging, but the folds thereof were heavy as perdurable lead. For all his strength, the warrior lad could not budge the fold of that curtain by a finger's breadth. He paused, panting, and searched the weird chamber with a frightened eye—and spied a second entranceway he had not at first perceived.

Of strange dark gold was this second doorway, and set terribly therein, like ghoulish and repulsive gems, were wet, glistening, naked human eyeballs.

From this terrible door he shrank in loathing. Slowly, painfully, labo-riously, the living eyes swiveled in their golden sockets to stare at him. There was an uncanny desperation in the gazing of those bodiless eyes. They stared at him with a horrible and an awful urgency. A message was in the fixed staring of those eyes, a poignant beseeching, an unspoken warning.

But no curtain, save impalpable shadow, barred his path.

Pressing white lips tight against a spasm of nausea, the lad shiver-ingly passed through the horrid doorway and found himself suddenly standing knee-deep in crimson gore!

Almost he sprang back—but then he realized, with a quaver of ter-rible relief, that it was but illusion.

He stood at one end of a long hall. The walls thereof were hung with a strange arras whereon a phantasmagoria of nameless and hybrid monstrosities coupled and cavorted, snarled and brayed, squirmed and battled, in a curious travesty of life.

The floor of this grim corridor was paved with a lucent stone the hue of freshly-shed human gore. Blood-red light beat up from this loathsome stone, bathing his feet in horrid luminance. His flesh crept on his bones as he stepped cautiously forward. It was like wading through hot, wet blood. Warmth was in this stone, and light was captive there, as if radiant atoms burned within the scarlet crystal. Shivering with revulsion, he strode grimly forward, but at every step he half-expected to feel the crawling moisture of hot fluid bathing his naked flesh.

Down the corridor of blood he passed, step by reluctant step, averting his eyes hastily from the half-alive obscenities that writhed and bellowed on the queer tapestry.

At the end of the gory hallway lay a door draped in the blackest and softest of velvets. Above, on the amber architrave of the portal, the emerald Eye of Phazdaliom glittered watchfully.

And Kellory half-knew what awaited him beyond the black curtain.

# CHAPTER 5

## THE THRONE OF THE SLEEPER

The dark curtains parted and he glided soundlessly through—to stop short, stifling the gasp that rose to his lips unbidden.

Silent as the grave and dark as death was this chamber. The walls were hung with a variety of nameless artworks. Intricate and curious and wonderful were they, seductive to the eye, conducive to meditation, and all were fashioned from substances of autumnal and somnolent hues. Rich old browns like the dregs of autumn ale; slumberous purples and darkening mauves; deep, slothful crimsons like cold and sluggish blood; vague and dreamy grays, like softest essence of shadows; and depthless, satiny blacks.

The chamber was floored with a night-dark crystal wherein, at amazing depths, small star-like points of icy fire were seemingly imbedded. To tread on this starry floor of black crystal was like walking across wintry skies.

Above, the ceiling rose to a peaked dome. Small lamps of starry silver hung by gemmy chains, and from these a thick and stifling incense fumed in slow coils of midnight-blue vapor. The dome was completely obscured with this perfumed smoke, and the air was heavy with slumberous fragrances.

But Kellory noted these things with but one single all-envisioning glance. His attention was riveted upon that which stood in the center of the chamber.

Picture a great, capacious throne hewn all from softly-glowing amber. The tree whose oozing veins had shed so vast a drop of congealing amber must have been as mighty a nemoral colossus as Yggdrasil itself.

Strewn with thick, strange, soft furs of deepest purple was this amberous throne.

And seated therein, as if overtaken by sleep amidst his brooding thoughts, a man sprawled motionless.

The blood pounding in his temples, scarce daring to breathe lest the faint susurration of an indrawn breath arouse the throned slumberer,

Kellory sank to a crouch on the floor of starry crystal, his hand going automatically to the hilt of his rude dagger. With alert and feral eyes, like a timorous beast, he took in the sleeper from crown to toe. For this, he knew, was Phazdaliom the Green Enchanter.

He wore the likeness of a young man, pale and delicate and slim; but Kellory knew that six centuries had passed since first this wan and epicene youth drew breath upon Zephrondus.

The sleeper had pallid and attenuated features, shadowed with melancholy. His face was pale and smooth as old wax, and time had drawn no harsh lines therein. Winged brows curved above translucent slumbering lids, as if etched with a delicate pencil. The long straight nose, the firm, mobile lips, the lean and delicate jaw were aristocratic, and touched with sorrow. Weariness sat on his pale smooth brow; there was languor and boredom in the sulky drooping of the full lips; a cryptic and profound reverie shadowed those features with a funereal sorrow.

His garments were somber and complicated, with many foldings and of an exquisite softness and delicacy of materials. The hues of these fantastical garments were all of green; but of a thousand subtly differing shades and tints of this primary color. Dark mystic greens like the shrouded fires that blaze in the cores of mighty emeralds; pallid hues of attenuated chartreuse; the lambent and lustrous green that shimmers in the scintillant eyes of feral and slinking cats; vibrant, vital greens that burn in the free foliage of springtime, and deep poisonous shades, the green of putrid and rotten flesh and the loathsome and deadly green of serpent-venom. Lucent and luminous tints, the greens of milky jade, and radiant chrysoprase, and apple-green chalcedony, and crystalline sparkling chrysoberyl.

One long slim hand, whereon strange talismanic rings glinted with dull fires, lay like the creamy petals of a dying lily along the curve of his thigh. The other drooped languidly over the massy arm of the luminous amber-yellow chair.

The sleeper made no slightest movement, and Kellory began to breathe again. Indeed, slumber lay so heavily upon the pale man with weary, jaded features that he seemed more like a corpse than one who merely slumbered. Layer upon layer of heavy, drugged slumber enwrapped him like dim, tenacious swathings of subtle shadow. He looked as if he had slumbered here for a thousand centuries of slow-moving time.

In the death-like stillness and funereal darkness of the chamber, whose dim air was heavy with drowsy, suffocating nard and opiate myrrh, Kellory felt his senses dull and his alertness waver. He felt, in his weariness, that he, too, might fall into a trance-like slumber in this inmost room whose every appurtenance and detail of decor was given over to the courting and the seduction of sleep. With a sharp effort, he snapped awake, digging the nails of his one good hand into his thigh so that the bite of pain would hold off the narcotic slumber that seemed about to envelop him.

Still the sleeper did not awake; slowly his fears were allayed and the tired boy began to relax. He was here where he had sought to come. Vengeance, like a burning and insatiable thirst raging within the very core of his being, had driven him to face all but unendurable perils, to come to stand in the presence of Phazdaliom.

Now—to do that for which he had dared and suffered so much.

He rose lithely to his feet, and approached the sleeper on silent naked feet. His left hand went out to touch the slumbering figure on his shoulder…it hung, hesitating…then it brushed the shoulder of the soft garments.

And the throne, and the figure within the throne, like an apparition— *vanished!*

# CHAPTER 6

## IN THE JAWS OF THE TRAP

Gone instantly, like a puff of vapor, throne and occupant winked out of existence. Kellory whirled to dart for the door, but he saw, in the next instant, and with a thrill of icy horror, that the chamber was no longer open. Unbroken, the wall stretched on all four sides! The door through which he had passed a moment before had vanished as swiftly and as magically as had the enthroned and somnolent Enchanter.

The panic of a trapped beast flamed up in the wild boy. Eyes afire, he spun about, snatching the dagger from the scabbard strapped to his slim bare thigh. Silvery light from the starry lamps glittered on the cold iron blade.

Softly, yet clearly, a languorous voice began speaking out of the empty air.

"Very foolish was it of you, Kellory, to dream you might with impunity venture into my citadel. No other mortal or immortal—of this world or the others—hath been so daring, or so impetuous, or so foolhardy, as to brave the many enchantments of this sanctum. Such courage, or such stupidity, astonishes me, youth. I would know the motive for your unparalleled intrusion—and it is for this reason alone that I hold in abeyance the many blasts of withering magic suspended about you. Answer swiftly and with candor, thou son of Thedric Ironmane, thou scion of the Black Wolf people, nor think that ever I shall permit you to leave this chamber living."

The voice spoke in cool, measured tones, wherein a weary boredom was manifest. Cultured and precise and musical was that low voice, but behind its drawling and melodious tones the ring of deadly and implacable menace could be sensed. Kellory had fallen into a fighting crouch. Now, but slowly and reluctantly, he rose to his full height, sliding the futile dagger back into its leathern sheath.

Quieting his hammering pulses, the half-grown, defenseless boy was silent while he mastered his fear—the vast and unmanning fear that had welled up within him at the first sound of that cold, polished and merciless voice.

"Come, child! Speak: you shall die painlessly and upon the instant, so reveal your motives without hesitation, for already my patience wanes. For seven hours I have been deep in abstruse and fascinating converse with a crystalloid intelligence inhabiting the frozen and sterile moon that encircles the planet Gulzund: your rash and importunate—and most unwelcome—invasion of this, my Chamber of Transcendental Communings, had discommoded me, and has earned for you mine enmity. My curiosity alone suspends—and that but momentarily—the swiftness of your doom. Therefore, boy, do not pursue your stubborn and obdurate silence any further, lest my impatience overcome and whelm my curiosity, to your bodily harm and spiritual detriment…"

There was a hint of mocking cruelty, a cold, cat-like flavor of malice, in the slow, measured, calm words. A cold finger touched Kellory's naked spine: never, he knew, in all his young years, had he stood closer to death than at this moment.

"Come, speak! You are a warrior's son, and no slinking thief, so I doubt me you have come hence in any vain attempt to steal my magical treasures; you are a princeling, if little more than a savage, so I doubt me you have crept hither as an assassin. I have worked no atrocity on your barbarian clan, so you come not to this place for any act of primitive vengeance. Speak: curiosity obsesses me!"

Kellory saw now that the whole chamber was one gigantic trap. Even though Phazdaliom slept in the deepest of ensorcelled and unhuman slumbers, his spirit in far and curious communion, watchful and unslumbering invisible forces had held the young intruder under continuous scrutiny, doubtless from the moment he had entered the enchanted palace. These unseen servants had whisked their master into some other plane of being at the first sign of physical danger. So much for his plans, his hopes, his caution and his braveries! He had nothing more to lose— since his life was already forfeit—so he might as well articulate the truth.

"I want you to teach me magic," the boy blurted.

# CHAPTER 7

## THE TALE OF KELLORY

After a moment of astonished silence, the voice of Phazdaliom made reply. Suave irony rang in the muted accents of his calm voice as he spake.

"Intellectual curiosity is ever to be encouraged, especially when found among the benighted savages of Barbaria," the Green Enchanter observed. "However, in all candor, I suspect the presence of a deeper motive behind your cunning and cautious trespass in the borders of my demesne than that of the thirst for knowledge."

Kellory shook his head stubbornly, wild locks flying.

"You are said to be the greatest sorcerer on all this world of Zephrondus," the boy said, "and I would learn from you the arts of magic!"

"Why?" demanded Phazdaliom, with a bluntness unusual for him.

The boy took a deep breath, marshalling his thoughts. He knew he was on trial for his life: thus the urgency of the moment drew from him an unwonted persuasiveness of phrasing.

"Listen to me," he said urgently. "Once my people ruled the shining city of Illyrion on the shores of Eryphon, the River of Dreams. High and golden was our empire; fair and lovely were our bright cities. But then, swarming down out of the Desolate Land, like a migration of crawling vermin, came the squat, ferocious, savage warriors of the Thungoda Horde in all their rapacious thousands. Our realm they overthrew, our fair and shining cities they trampled beneath their iron-shod hooves, and those few of us who escaped the slaughter survived but as half-naked savages in the barren wilderness."

"Regrettably true," the suave Enchanter murmured. "But these things are ancient history, child…"

Again, Kellory shook his head.

"Now they drift down south of these, the Nykranian Mountains, into the southern lands of Sarkovy. First in few and scattered war parties; but soon in all their numberless thousands they will descend, from realm to realm across the world, smothering all civilization under the weight of their Horde." He lifted his right hand, that which wore the glove of black leather.

"I am the last of the Black Wolves," he said grimly. "They let me live, a helpless boy, because of the momentary whim of their cruel warlord. But my father and all my clan they crushed into the mire. And before they permitted me to flee, they held this, my right hand, in the flames of the torture-fire until it was a dead and useless thing. This they did so that never could I bear a sword against them. So be it: but my *left* hand can still brandish and employ the Staff of a wizard; and as I fled sobbing and alone into the wilderness, I swore on the death of my father that if I could not battle the crawling Thungoda vermin as a warrior I should go up in war against them with all the powers of a magician. Hence am I come here to your fire-moated palace, to plead for your assistance. Let me be your chela! Teach to me the Arts of Darkness, O Phazdaliom!"

The boy's strident and extraordinary speech held the sure ring of conviction and truth in it. And there ensued a lengthy silence as the Enchanter pondered his words. At last he spoke again, musing and thoughtful:

"I shall not pretend to be moved by your appeal, child, for it is based on sentiment and emotion, and these appurtenances of mortality I have long since foresworn. While your motives would seem sincere and altruistic, I see as yet no reason why I should disturb the even tenor of my days and abandon the mystic studies which I have pursued for six centuries of time, to tutor a naked and illiterate savage boy."

"Have you no love for men, your brothers?" the boy cried.

"None whatsoever; neither have my 'brothers,' as you term them, any particular affection for me or my colleagues of the Brotherhood of Darkness," the Enchanter answered coldly. "I have turned from the company of mankind for centuries and see naught to my advantage in admitting a single member of the sorry species into intimate intercourse with my secret arts." Tears stung Kellory's eyes. Fiercely he blinked them back, searching his mind desperately for some argument that would win the Enchanter to his cause. At last an inspiration flashed before his mind; it was a chancy appeal to pin his hopes upon, but cogitation could produce no better.

"I have heard," he blurted boldly, "that a magician may hold Time the Destroyer at bay for seven centuries, no more. Would you go down into the Kingdom of Shadows with no man in all the world to know, or to mourn, of your passing? Teach me your occult science, O Phazdaliom, and let me go forth as a wizard at war against the vile Thungoda! I shall sweep them from the earth, and men shall honor my name forever. Bards shall sing an epic of my deeds for as long as the world shall last…and, forever after, in future time, when men shall speak of Kellory...shall the name of Phazdaliom, his master, be far from their lips?"

He finished his last appeal and stood there panting and exhausted, waiting for the Enchanter to answer. But no reply came to his final words. The chamber lay in dense silence for a very long time.

At last, and wearily, the voice of Phazdaliom spoke:

"Ah, child, what arts of persuasion you learned at the breast of your savage mother! Know that you have touched a secret and melancholy sorrow within me...for long have I mused on the futility of my magister-hood: what use to conquer the Nine Arts of the Secret Science, when after my inevitable and destined end, no man shall know the breadth of my sorcerous accomplishments?"

"Then—you will accept me into your service?" the boy asked tremu-lously, scarce daring to breathe, so vast was the hope that rose within him.

A weary chuckle answered him. Then: Then, and briskly: "A portal shall now open in the wall to your left: therein you will find a bath of hot and scented water; bathe well, boy, for uncleanliness offends my fastidiousness. And don the raiment my unseen servitors shall distribute beside the pool: your body is indecently uncovered. Then we shall have to see what we can do to teach you some familiarity with letters...alas, you have so very much to learn, and little time is left to me on this plane of being! Hurry, now—and put some order in those matted locks. There will be a comb somewhere, I suppose..."

The Enchanter's voice died away in fretful mutterings, and the relief was so great that Kellory staggered and almost fell. But, mastering his weakness, he stood tall and proud as the doorway melted into vacuity.

"Yes—Master!" he said, and went from the room to investigate the unfamiliar mysteries of bathing.

\* \* \* \*

And thus it was that the boy, Kellory, the son of Thedric Ironmane and the last living descendent of the Lost Kings of Illyrion, became ap-prenticed to Phazdaliom the Green Enchanter in his dark palace atop the sky-tall crest of Yothlymbris the Mountain of Fire, in the land of the Nykranian Mountains.

# PART 2

## IN THE VALLEY OF SILENCE

# CHAPTER 1

## GREEN EYES

From the gates of Grand Khev the road stretches east across the open grassy plains of Sarkovy to the mountains. From thence, it twists and crawls like a dusty gray serpent through the foothills, rising ever higher and higher to the Arul Pass. It was there, at the height of the pass, that Carthalla came to the end of her strength and fell to her knees in the sharp stones.

All day she had run behind the shaggy, horned ponies of her captors. It was soon after dawn that the Thungoda war party had attacked the company of a dozen knights her father had sent to escort her on her way. The ugly little men in greasy furs had lain hidden in the tall grasses. They rose to their feet, loosing a shower of barbed arrows on the astonished knights, and sprang howling upon them, pulling them down one by one.

Carthalla alone they spared. The reason was obvious: she was a woman—young, fresh and beautiful.

They lashed her wrists together with a leathern thong and galloped off toward the mountains. She was forced to run on foot in the dust of their hooves. If she fell, and she fell several times, she must scramble to her feet again however she might, and go on, or lie and be dragged to death.

The life of a Prince's daughter is luxurious and silken. Carthalla had never known fatigue, save as a languid weariness after an all-night ball. Nor had she ever known pain, save as a small discomfort or a childish illness soon dispelled by her father's court physician. But now she knew such pain and weariness as she never dreamed flesh could endure.

Her lungs ached as if on fire. Every breath she drew with dry, sobbing lips was agony. The furious torment of the tight thongs about her wrists soon died to a numbness. But it was her feet and legs—*there* was pain, pain beyond thought. Her fashionable riding-boots of Ordovic leather had seized the fancy of the squat, leering little Thungoda leader: so he had stripped them from her legs, leaving her feet bare. The long road was harsh and cindery with the height of summer. And her slim little feet were soft and tender. Soon, very soon, they were bruised and sore. Ere long they left a wet, red trail in the road-dust.

But now, as they came almost to the crest of the pass, she could go no farther. She fell to her knees, crying out sharply as the thongs bit cruelly into her swollen wrists. But the Thungoda did not stop. They dragged her through the dust, and the one to whose horned horse she was tethered turned and grinned back. Her gown was torn and disarranged from the pawing of dirty Thungoda hands, when they had searched her for gems. Now, through the rents in the long skirt, her bare limbs gleamed white. Sharp rocks gashed her thighs and knees. Harsh road-dust rasped her tender flanks, leaving them raw.

In her exhaustion and torment and despair, she called aloud on her god. His name was Changlamar. A little god of the sea was he, and seldom worshipped in these dark days. But it was his Sign had reigned at her nativity, and the Prince her father had vowed her to his phratry.

She called, then, out of the depths of her hopelessness. Nor did she expect an answer.

But then the horned horse stopped.

She lay wearily in the dust, bedrabbled with blood, gasping with dust-smirched lips for breath. It was no use: she could not rise; let them kill her here. Or rape her, or do to her whatever things the brutal Thungoda did to the Sarkovian women they seized. But none came to boot her to her feet. Instead, she heard the warriors muttering to each other ahead. She lifted her head from the dust of the road and peered forward.

It was nearly sundown and the immense curve of the sky was dim crimson fire. Against the dark flame of the sky, ahead of them at the crest of the pass, stood a tall man.

She could not see him clearly, for the light was dim and her eyes were watering from the dust. But he was no Thungoda: six feet and more was he, tall and lean, and straight as a spear. His sinewy limbs were naked under the tunic of supple black leather cinched in at the waist with a girdle of iron plates.

Heavy bands of iron clasped his right wrist and his upper arm. He wore boots, but no spurs. And a huge black cloak with batwinged collar flapped in the rising wind about him.

He stood silent, grim, looking them over: the nine mounted Thungoda warriors, who eyed him belligerently, yet uneasily, as they fingered their sword-hilts; and the helpless girl with yellow hair who sprawled in the dust of the road, and who raised wondering eyes in a pleading gaze to his. He neither moved nor spoke for a time: he stood, leaning on a tall iron-shod Staff of heavy black wood, regarding them with strange burning eyes set in a dark, clean-shaven and impassive face.

His eyes. They were the first odd thing Carthalla noticed about him. In her father's realm of Sarkovy, people had blue or gray eyes. But his were *green*—cold, burning eyes of weird green flame. They blazed in his dark-skinned, gaunt face. It was hard, that face, too harsh and somber to be handsome. A long thin white scar crooked down from his hairline to his black, scowling brows. She shivered involuntarily as the gaze of those burning green eyes paused to rest momentarily on her, before lifting to bend their lambent scrutiny upon her uneasy captors.

And then she saw his hand. His right hand. It wore a glove of black leather; but the left hand, that clasped the black Staff, went bare.

Then she noticed yet a third odd thing about him. He had the hard, dangerous look of a warrior, but he was none, for he wore no sword—not even an empty scabbard. Nor—now that she thought of it—was his thick black hair woven into a warrior's single braid. Instead, it swung loose about his lean face in a tangle of witchlocks, stirring to the touch of the wind, which had suddenly turned chill.

He loomed like an apparition against the dark flame of the sky. One lone man, unarmed; yet there was something about him that held the Thungoda back. They chittered uneasily amongst themselves, casting half-frightened, half-challenging glances at him from their squinting, slitted eyes. Any other man who stood in their path, they would have ridden down, whooping and slashing with curved steel. This man…they did not like to face. It was all very curious.

It was even a little frightening.

# CHAPTER 2

## THE BLACK WOLF

Kugal, chief of the Thungoda war party, felt his prestige ebb as he hesitated before the grim, dark man who blocked their path. He reined his horned horse forward, drawing his curved sword.

"Who are you, man?" he demanded harshly, letting him see naked steel.

"I am Kellory," the stranger said in a low voice. And: "Release the girl."

*"Hai!"* Kugal crowed, grinning. "One man—no steel—and you give orders to Thungoda!" He laughed, thin lips peeling back to reveal discolored tusks. Then, in the way of his Horde, his temper changed. He snarled, spitting viciously, and suddenly his narrow slitted eyes were cold with venom.

"I cut your guts out with this," he spat, showing Kellory the sword again, "and make you eat them!"

Kellory did not move. His green eyes were wintry and his voice was as low as a whisper as he said:

"Set the girl free and go your way, Thungoda. Or you shall kneel at the feet of Pnom in the Kingdom of Shadows before the world's an hour older."

It was not a boast; not even a threat. There was the quiet ring of certitude to his words. It was a promise.

Kugal grimaced, and spat again, and made his shaggy-maned steed rear a little. He should have squalled a war cry and ridden the tall man down. But, somehow, he didn't. He didn't even try.

"You Sarkovyman?" he demanded.

Kellory shook his head, witchlocks tangling. "I am a man of the North," he said impassively.

"Barbarian?"

Kellory's eyes blazed up at an old memory.

"My people were the Black Wolf nation," he said softly. "The Thungoda Horde butchered them to the last babe ten years since. I have never forgotten the face of the leader, Mnar."

Kugal grinned again.

"Prince Mnar? He rules all Thungoda now. He cut down Black Wolves of Thedric Ironmane: soon all Sarkovy fall to steel of Thungoda, like this girl. City Khev run red with blood of Sarkovymen. We kill all—all!"

His greasy, swart face flushed dark at the thought of the blood to come. Kugal was no longer intimidated by the somber mien and burning witch-eyes of the tall man. Suddenly, without a moment's warning, he jerked his horned horse forward and swung at Kellory's face, steel flashing in the sunset light.

Lightning flared!

Blinding, dazzling, a blaze of intolerable blue-white light flashed from the black wood Staff in Kellory's hand. The spark of lightning caught the curved sword as it swung for his face. In a splatter of flying droplets of molten steel, the saber flew from Kugal's hand. He was dead from the bolt before he had time to scream, sprawling under the heels of his own horse, which bucked and jumped from the nearness of the dark man, fled back down the pass, blundering into the eight other Thungoda warriors, knocking them this way and that. Struggling with the reins, snatching at sword-hilts, squalling and spitting with fury and surprise, they lurched against the sides of the pass. And flash after flash from the black Staff lit the gloomy way as Kellory struck them down.

It was over almost as soon as it had begun. Nine twisted corpses lay huddled against the rough stone. The fresh air of early evening was heavy with the stench of burnt man-flesh, and the weird metallic odor of ozone hung on the wind.

Kellory strode to where Carthalla lay frozen and cut her bonds. She stared up at him, her pale, dust-smeared face white with shock, her enormous eyes filled with disbelief.

"Are you wizard...or warrior?" she whispered handy.

"I am both," he said, helping her to her feet. He used only his left hand in so doing, leaning the black Staff against the rocky wall of the pass. His right hand, which wore the glove if black leather, was inert and stiff.

"Can you walk, or shall I carry you?" he grunted.

"To where?"

He nodded in the direction.

"There is a cave up under the ledges of the cliff. I will make a fire. Night will be upon us soon, and these are the Ghoul-Haunted Hills. Come—let me help you."

And then great winds awoke and rose, and shouldered aside the thick-piled clouds, and showed forth great bright furnaces of sunset gold.

# CHAPTER 3

## "MY NAME IS VENGEANCE!"

When Carthalla woke next morning, she was alone in the cave. The fire had burned to cold ash sometime in the night but she had slept warmly in the furs he had given her. With a little shiver, the girl recalled the weird manner with which Kellory had made the fire. He had simply laid his left hand on the pile of wood—the left hand, which wore a small iron ring on the middle finger, a ring engraven with a glyph in no language she had ever seen—and he had spoken a Word. And fire blazed up! It was uncanny. She wondered idly, stretching and yawning under the warm furs, why he had not used his terrible black Staff—his "blasting wand," as he called it. If it could melt the Thungoda chieftain's sword like a lightning bolt, surely it could set the twigs afire. But, then, perhaps too much fire was worse than none at all; perhaps the lightnings of the Staff could not be so finely controlled; and had he been so foolish as to use the Staff, the cave might have been shattered to rubble. She shivered again. What a strange, grim man he was!

At length she stirred and got up. It was the custom of Sarkovy for men and women to sleep naked, but she had slept in the torn remnants of her gown, since she did not wish to bare her body before Kellory. She had expected to be raped and murdered by the Thungoda warriors who had seized her on the road; escaping their lusts, she did not wish to risk her maidenhead by tempting the manhood of the strange silent man who had saved her. He was not of Sarkovy; he was not even a warrior, or at least he did not wear his hair in a warrior's braid. Sarkovy women are taught to despise the touch of foreign men—even those who, like herself, a Prince's daughter, are expected to wed foreign Princes. And, anyway, she did not like Kellory. She was used to the gallant, laughing young knights and nobles of Grand Khev: with their fresh, fair coloring and bright blue eyes and golden hair. This Black Wolf—he was aptly born!— was too harsh and grim, too dark and cold and hard for her tastes. She felt a small delicious shiver run over her at the thought of those strong hard hands on her body—and that right hand, gloved in black, and useless.

Thinking of Kellory made Carthalla wonder where he was. For he was not in the small cave, and the black cloak, whereon he had lain all night at her side, was gone. Surely he had not departed! Why, today he was going to take her back to the court of her father—or so, at least, she expected.

She found him sitting outside the cave mouth, staring down at the dim plains through the blur of morning mist. His Staff lay beside him, ready to his hand. His arms were wrapped around his knees, and his brooding face rested upon them, as he stared thoughtfully down at the land of Sarkovy spread out to the dawn.

"I feared you might have gone, and left me," she said, when it became obvious he had not noticed her standing behind him. He grunted something. But he did not turn to greet her, and neither did he rise up from his place.

She cleared her throat tentatively. Then, after a moment or two of silence, the girl came over and sat down awkwardly near where he crouched.

"Where is Grand Khev?" she inquired after a time, more to break the silence and open a conversation than to gain the fact.

He gestured with the gloved hand.

"There," he grunted.

"My father will be astonished when I return home," she said. "He would have thought me halfway to Aijan by now."

"Why were you going to Aijan, anyway?" he asked. "We talked but little last night, you were so tired."

She busied her hands, trying to get her bright hair neat.

"I am trothed to the Prince of Aijan," she said coolly, "and yesterday was my seventeenth birthday. Since I am now of age, my father, the Prince Valemyr, dispatched me to the court of my future husband, the Prince Shio. Oh, my father will be enraged when he hears how the Thungoda attacked our party scarce an hour's ride from the city gates! Never have I known the Thungoda to dare strike so close to Khev. They grow bolder. It is time the knights of Valemyr taught them a lesson." His emerald gaze brooded on the mist-drenched land below.

He nodded towards the plains of Sarkovy, witchlocks stirring.

"Not Valemyr, but Fear, is king over this land," he said.

She raised her head to look at him with surprise. He went on, after a moment:

"It is time that Valemyr and all the Seven Princes of Sarkovy realized the truth," he said. "For a hundred years now, the Thungoda have been drifting down from the North. First they came in small war parties, and scarce ventured south of Ulgoth River. Then in larger and ever larger parties. Then they stayed, some of them, building their wood-walled *mengli*. They settled far from the Seven Cities, and no one cared: the pains of Sarkovy are vast, and there is room for all—or so the Princes thought, the fools!"

Anger flashed briefly in Carthalla's wide blue eyes. She tossed her head a little, bright hair catching the sun.

"Why 'fools'?" she demanded.

"Because they confuse that which they *wish* to be true with that which *is* true," he replied harshly. "The Thungoda are here to stay. And they are only the vanguard. Millions more will follow, and one by one the great stone cities will go down before them, unless one of the Princes moves against them now."

Anger made red patches burn in her cheeks.

"Of course *you* are wiser than the Lords of Sarkovy!" she observed tartly. He turned his cold green gaze on her. But there was no anger in his voice when he spoke.

"Listen, girl. I was born beyond those mountains you see marching like a purple wall to the north—in the land you city-dwellers speak of, contemptuously, as Barbaria. Well, a hundred years before the first Thungoda parties began seeping through the mountains into Sarkovy, they began drifting into my homeland, too, and in the same manner: first scattered parties, then whole tribes. They came down from the ultimate North, out of the Desolate Land. And they came to stay. First they built their palisaded camps, their mengli. Then they decided to take hold of a city—"

"Are there cities in Barbaria?" she asked, almost tauntingly. Again this detestable, cold, hard man refused to rise to the bait.

"There were cities in the North when all *this* land was empty fields," he said grimly. "Surely you have heard of Illyrion, the City of the High Kings?"

She bridled a little.

"Yes…of course! I had forgotten that Lost Illyrion was a northern city…but that was long before Barbaria was—Barbaria!"

He ignored this.

"The city they took was called Amyris, the White City. It was famous for its poets and philosophers. Old statues of mellow ivory dreamed in the purple shadows of the long arcades of Amyris, and the great Theatre, where once the plays of Kesirion and Scoupher were first performed, could hold ten thousand citizens. The Thungoda turned the White City red with the blood of the slaughtered. They hacked the ivory statues of the Kings to pieces; they fired the Golden House to rubble; the great bowl of the Theatre they used for an arena and pitted the legions that had surrendered to their lies against man-dragons and theladars captured on the black shores of the Kynellarian Sea. There was not one man, woman or child alive in Amyris when they were done with their red work. Thus it will be with Sarkovy, too, in time."

She did not say anything. He noticed that the color had drained from her face.

He went on.

"We fought them. For sixty years, we fought them. But it was too late by then. The time to fight was when they were but few, and scattered. We, in our vanity and foolishness, had let ninety thousand warriors of the Thungoda Horde enter into our land. And they crushed us. City by city, castle by castle, tribe by tribe. My people were a tribe of half-naked savages when I was born: but my father's father had been High King of Illyrion. You may have heard of him, if you paid any attention to your tutors: Niodronicus, seventh of that name."

"Niodronicus of the Glory?" she whispered faintly. He nodded, and his eyes were cold and somber.

"Even as savage tribesmen they would not let us live in the land which had once been ours, and which had now become theirs," he continued. "Tribe by tribe they crushed us into the mire. They breed like rats in the sewers: there were an hundred forty thousand of them by that time. My people, the Black Wolf nation, were the last to go under. My father had led us into the hills at the edge of the mountains. We were hard to find, and harder yet to fight. But they found us, and they fought us. They have no reverence for life. They will spend the lives of a hundred warriors to drag down a single man of your people or of mine. In the end, they had us all. My brothers they spitted on pikes, and those that were too young to walk yet were tossed alive into the torture-fires. My father they flayed before my eyes, before they burnt him alive. *My mother*—"

His lips clamped together against the terrible words. They were white from the pressure. She did not dare to meet his eyes: the withering blaze in them was not human. And she cursed her wanton tongue that had taunted and baited him earlier.

He went on, in a very low tone.

"Only I lived. They let me live. It was a whim of their warlord, Mnar: him that is now their Prince. I remember how he sat on his black stallion, the light of burning men flickering on the polished steel of his spiked helm, grinning down at the last of the line of ancient kings—a naked, frightened boy of ten, bound and helpless in the dust. 'Let one live,' he laughed—I will hear that laugh until the hour I perish from the world—'let one live, to remember our clemency.' *Clemency!*" He spat, as if the word was slime in his mouth.

"What—happened then?" she asked in a faint whisper.

"They let me loose," he growled. "But first they held my hand—my right hand—my *sword* hand—in the fire till it was black and dead. It was so that I could never bear a sword against them, they said. It was the fire my father was dying in. He yet lived—a little. He looked down at me from the stake, and he breathed out one word: *live!* He spoke in the Old Tongue, so the swine could not understand. The pain in my hand was very great. I had never known such pain. But I remember the rage and the fury in his eyes, and the sorrow in them, and the pride. And I whispered one word so that he could hear it as he died. I said *kel-lor-ri.* It is the Old Tongue, and its meaning is: *I will avenge.*"

"Your name…"

He shook his head, witchlocks blowing about his lean jaw. "I had another name then. An old and proud name: kings had borne it once. But now my name is Vengeance."

He turned his cold, brooding gaze upon the girl who sat pale and silent at his side, there on the rocky ledge overlooking the plains of Sarkovy.

"And now you know why I cannot spare the time to take you back to Khev. I have been watching since dawn. There are three hundred warriors of the Horde down on those plains between here and the city. My Power is not strong enough to permit the two of us to fight through them—*yet.* But soon I will be strong enough, aye, powerful enough to reach into the City of Terror and pull down Black Mnar from his high place and send his foul spirit down to squeal and flop on the red-hot floors of hell, where it belongs! Soon—very soon now, if my god is with me, I shall become the greatest sorcerer that this world has seen since the high days of old…"

"What do you mean?"

"With this useless hand, I could not become a warrior. So I became a wizard—a *Warlock,* warrior and wizard combined in one man. Old Phazdaliom the Green Enchanter was my teacher: I came to him a naked, crippled savage. He taught me the Nine Arts and thus I entered into the Brotherhood of Darkness."

Carthalla had heard of the Brotherhood of Darkness, the ancient and worldwide fellowship of sorcerers. Great was their power and their mastery over the Invisible World that lies beyond this world of the living, but she also had heard that initiates of the Brotherhood of Darkness are sworn on terrible oaths never to employ their dreadful power to meddle in the flow of world history. She said as much, and Kellory nodded.

"True. But my need is great. I shall go up in war against the Thungoda filth, and I shall tread them down under my heel. If I cannot do it with the Sword, I shall do it with the Staff! And the gods may do with my miserable spirit what they will, in the end."

His voice was hoarse, as hard and dry as crumbling desert rocks under the baking skies of the desert.

And not for the first time that day, Carthalla found herself shivering in the cold grim presence of this dark and terrible man.

# CHAPTER 4

## THE RIDE TO BLACK RIVER

The sun was high in the noonward sky before Kellory would turn aside to break their fast and rest a little. They had ridden all morning on the shaggy little horn-horses Kellory had tethered in the pass. These were the horses of the Thungoda war party from whom he had rescued Carthalla yesterday at sunset: but the Thungoda would ride them no more.

When they set out, he had explained the mission whereon he was bound. Once (he said), ages ago, there had been a mighty magician by the name of Yaohim. "Lord of Shadows," his name meant, in the Old Tongue, for he alone possessed mastery of a secret art. This art he had used once against the Sea Devils when they had come thundering down Turisan River to loot and ravage and burn.

Carthalla had heard vaguely of the Sea Devils. They were wild and savage and bloody corsairs who had infested the Hundred Isles that lay many leagues off the shores of Sarkovy in the midst of the great green sea. Their lean black galleys had glided by night through the deep but narrow river, and dawn found them at the walls of Gorovod, first and eldest of the Seven Cities. In their thousands, the wild corsairs took the city by storm. But Amric, Prince of Gorovod, fled by a secret way and rode with a small band of followers seven nights and seven days across the plains of Sarkovy, giving warning to his brother Princes that the Sea Devils had landed in great force and were sworn to pull down the Seven Cities, one by one.

South of Grand Khev the Black River crawls like a sluggish stream of pitch from the southernmost of the mountains. And somewhere, beyond Black River, dwelt Yaohim the Lord of Shadows. The master magician was no friend to the Princes of Sarkovy, but he well knew that if the cities fell, all they who dwelt in this land would go in peril of their lives—even a magician.

So he rode back to whelmed and broken Gorovod with Amric at his side. Within the stone-walled city, the devil pirates of the Hundred Isles feasted and swilled red wine and tortured and raped, not knowing the hour of their Doom was upon them. And that night, in the dark of the three moons, Yaohim worked a mighty feat of shadow magic. No man knows what he did nor what followed upon his calling, but with dawn a sight of horror met the eyes of Prince Amric and his men.

Six thousand corsairs had swilled and sung within the walls of Gorovod with sunset. With dawn, six thousand madmen mewled and tittered in the ravaged halls.

And, withouten thanks nor payment, the Lord of Shadows had ridden back to his tower beyond Black River and vanished from the memory of men.

But Kellory remembered.

He reasoned that a magic strong enough to whelm the wild pirates of the Isles in all their bloody thousands could strike down the numberless warriors of the Thungoda Horde as well.

Thus was he bound for the tower of the magician, or whatever remained thereof. For among the ruins of the tower (his tutor and master had whispered) lay to this hour the Grimoire of Yaohim, the Book of Shadows, wherein the secret of this mighty magic lay.

And Kellory would find it or die.

There was something of the gallant and the heroic in this lonely quest of one man for a secret that could destroy the foul and numberless vermin that imperiled the world. Carthalla felt the thrill of it: this was the stuff of songs. Whether Kellory the Warlock won or lost, someday the bards would sing of his long quest, that now was nearly done.

…Save that, if he lost, the Thungoda would leave alive no bards to sing nor Sarkovymen to listen to that song.

Nor did she mind any longer that he would not turn aside from his quest to return her to the city of her father. At first, hearing that she must ride with him or be left behind to fare as she might, she had railed and ranted. To her tears and threats alike, Kellory had remained unmoved. To him it was very simple: they could not fight their way through the war parties that now infested the road between the pass and Grand Khev. To detour far to the south was the only safe way. And south lay the region whereunto he was bound, on a mightier and more important mission than merely bringing a lost girl home to her father's hearth, be she princess or no.

And, since they must go south in any case, why not finish the quest and bring forth the Book of Shadows ere riding to the gates of Khev? It was perfectly simple.

And, to tell the truth, something within the girl's heart responded to the plan. How glorious it would be to ride into Khev, bearing the salvation of the world! How pleased her father would be, and how proud of her. She knew him well: a good man, but not overly strong. His land lay in peril from the numberless Thungoda that swarmed in ever-increasing hordes across the plains. And he knew it well, and worried over it. But the cities of Sarkovy were few, as yet. Men were new-come into these plains: only five centuries before, Roldomar the Mighty had led the peoples into Sarkovy from the lost realm of the South, long-since overrun by the Ghost Legions loosed during the Wizard's War of the last age, when the Gold City fell before the Witchmen. As yet, the warriors of Sarkovy were too few to face in battle the Thungoda—even were the Seven Princes to become convinced of the ever-growing peril.

Thus, as they lunched on Kellory's packet of dried meats and black Cryphax wine, the girl became enwrapped deeper and deeper in the vision of the glory to come when she rode with Kellory and the Book under the frowning battlements of Grand Khev, to lead the knights of Sarkovy to a magnificent victory over the brutish little beastmen of the Horde.

They mounted and rode on.

By starfall they had passed Black River at the ancient ford. With the rising of Diostrion, the Emerald Moon, they made camp. That night they slept on the brink of the Valley of the Wizard.

# CHAPTER 5

## THE CRAWLING SLIME

When dawn came shouldering up over the edges of the world, and flooded the landscape with pale gold fight, Carthalla went down to the banks of the Black River without bothering to awaken her companion. She was filthy with the dust and grime of travel, and her body stank of sour sweat. She *must* bathe, and be the water black or no, at least it was wet. In the shelter of overhanging ferns she stripped off her filthy gown, which was by now little more than rags. She handled it despairingly. She would scrub it as clean as possible—but later. First the bath. However, she could not resist ripping the remnants of the hem away: from thigh down the gown was in long ribbons which entangled her legs when she walked. So she tore the soiled cloth and made an abbreviated, but more travel-worthy, garment from what was left. Then, with a heartfelt sigh of pleasure, she waded through the rushes and slid into the cold, wet caress of the ebon waters.

For a time she drifted, swimming idly, blissfully enjoying the intimate touch of the cold water. Strange beyond telling was this river: black as ink its waters, and no man knew why, though some said it flowed up out of the Kingdom of Shadows at the bottom of the world, the place where the shadows of dead men went who were not welcome in the higher world of the gods…

Then a cold hand closed around her ankle and she screamed!

Another hand locked around her left wrist, and a long slick limb or member—it felt like a serpent—slid around her waist. Carthalla went wild with terror and shrieked again and again, kicking frantically and beating the water in a desperate effort to free herself from the embrace of the unknown thing beneath the black waters. But it clung with incredible strength and when, with wild effort, she dragged her left hand above the surface she saw with an indescribable thrill of horror that a rope of moving slime was locked about it!

Like some vile grayish jelly it was, and transparent, for the light struck through it if but dimly. The very touch of the slime thing against her flesh was loathsome, and she fought it with every strength in her young body.

Luckily, she had not ventured very far out into Black River. Her feet still touched bottom, and with this for leverage she somehow managed to struggle nearer in to shore, so that she stood partway out of the water. Looking down, she saw with a gasp of terror and revulsion the thing that held her in its unbreakable grip.

A gigantic mass of quaking, blubbery slime met her eyes. It had no limbs, no head, no eyes. Somehow it could shape extensions of itself, and three of these long tentacle-like extrusions of hard jelly were looped about her. Even as she watched, bulges appeared in the glistening, smooth surface of the slime thing. They grew out like nipples—then extended farther, like wriggling feelers. She knew they would grow larger and become yet more arms to ensnare her and drag her down to a hideous death on the murky floors of Black River.

Suddenly, Kellory was there.

Her cries had awakened him and he had sprung to his feet in answer to her call so swiftly that he had not thought to seize up his blasting wand. Now as he saw the jelly thing that had already half-enveloped the naked, struggling girl, a wild black rage awoke within him.

He lifted up his arms to the morning skies and cried in a great voice:

"Go back down, *shioggua!* Go back down. I am a Warlock of the Secret Flame. My circle is the Ninth; my sphere the Sphere of Darkness; my god is Azzamungandyr the Lord of the Mysteries. *You—may—not—take—the—girl!"*

It seemed to Carthalla almost as if the quivering mass of slime had ears and could hear his words. It—hesitated. It—waited. And it seemed to her that Kellory was grown greater than before: his Power enveloped him like a mighty mantle he could draw on at will.

But the slime monster did not obey. It did not withdraw. Seeing this, Kellory drew in his breath and called upon the inmost resources of his being—hidden wells of strength few mortal men ever disturb. There within him, deeply hidden, as it lies hidden within every man, is a Power which links him to the unseen maze of forces and alignments that constitutes the Plenum—the Totality, the All, the Complete Universe of Space and Time. He called now upon that Power: few men dare call upon it; but he dared.

It seemed to Carthalla that his face and figure darkened to utter blackness. In this blackness his weird green eyes burned like emerald suns—blazing with intolerable brilliance. The sky above him grew dark, though it was day. He seemed to grow taller—taller—beyond the height of man. Like a tower of ultimate darkness he loomed up into the sky, and his eyes were like great windows that looked in upon the seething flames of hell.

"Go back down, *shioggua!* This woman is mine! You may not take her for your foul pleasure. Need I call upon the Timeless Ones—the Guardians of the Balance? I speak the Name ASSATHYAIOQQUN-QUANDAR! ZAOTH! PHUOL LUMNIVUUR! Go back down, Foulness, lest I smite thee with the Secret Flame!"

Thunder cracked in the pitch-black night above them, and sulphurous flames of no lightning ever seen by man licked at the edges of the roiling black clouds.

But suddenly the thing was gone. The slime slid back into the depths of Black River and Carthalla stood free.

Suddenly she was very conscious of her body, with the eyes of Kellory upon her. She crooked one forearm across her full young breasts and covered her lap with the palm of her other hand, in the immemorial posture of woman surprised.

But Kellory—now no longer sky-tall and terrible—was no longer looking at her. His dark, lean face was pale and drawn and it glistened wetly. He looked, suddenly, exhausted to the point of collapse. Indeed, he staggered and almost fell to his knees.

Her modesty forgotten, Carthalla came up out of the water and seized his arm.

"What is wrong? Are you hurt?" she cried. He tried to speak but could not; then, all at once, his full weight was against her and she saw that he had swooned. Could it be the feat of magic that had so greatly unmanned him? Staggering under his dead weight, the girl half-carried and half-dragged him back to their camp. She wished that she knew more about magic, and the ways of magicians.

A little wine revived him, although he still looked pale and drawn. His green eyes were strangely colorless, empty and without their usual fire, as he looked up, thanking her with a long glance. She smiled back, anxiously: she had not bothered to retrieve her gown, but had wrapped her wet body in his long black warlock-cloak.

"I will be all right," he said hoarsely.

"What was that—that *thing?*" Carthalla asked with a little grimace of revulsion.

"A *shioggua*—a Guardian Demon, summoned from the Water Element. Old Yaohim left his land…protected."

She shivered uncontrollably, perhaps from the morning wind on her wet nakedness under the cloak, or perhaps from the memory of that dread embrace. "It was…horrible!"

He nodded weakly. Then the faint shadow of a smile crossed his hard mouth.

"Now you know better than to bathe in Black River," he said.

# CHAPTER 6

## THE VALLEY OF SILENCE

Towards mid-morn they reached the wizard's tower. A little rest and some wine and food had restored Kellory's strength—or most of it. Only he knew how terribly his reserves of Power had been drained in fighting off the *shioggua.* He dreaded the next adversary, for surely the Lord of Shadows had left more than one Guardian to stand watch over his demesne.

But—and this was very odd—they met with no more supernatural encounters on their path. Kellory found this disquieting in the extreme. Surely, an Air Elemental should have been set to watch over the treasures of Yaohim. Or, most terrible of all, a Demon of the Earth, with the iron mineral strength of the earth itself slumbering in its vast, misshapen limbs. But no other Being accosted them, and they went forward into the morning.

The valley was silent and dim, for all the blaze of noon above. Tall trees shadowed the path, but no birds sang in their branches and the leaves rustled not in the breeze. It was as if a Spell of Silence had been set over the wizard's vale. Kellory did not like it at all.

Perhaps (he thought) the force he had aroused when he put forth his full Power and called upon That which is not summoned lightly had driven the other Guardians into hiding. The inhabitants of the Invisible World have senses other than the nine known to him. The release of such Power as he had summoned forth disturbs the equilibrium of the Other World, and dark things far from the site of such a calling-forth are made aware of it: as a stone thrown into a pond sends ripples travelling to the farthest shores of a lake. Perhaps this was the answer.

Perhaps...

And then the tower of Yaohim stood before them, dark and tall and forbidding in the blaze of noon sun.

Most curiously, although more than three hundred years must have passed since the death of the master magician, his tower yet stood unshaken by the tides of time. He paused, and stopped, and stood there for a time, frowning thoughtfully on the tower of Yaohim. For seven years he had striven to stand in this place. For although his master, Phazdaliom, had known much of the history of the Lord of Shadows, he had not known where in the wide-wayed world his wizard's fortress stood. Long and hard had Kellory searched in the years since he had left the castle of Phazdaliom; far to the east had he gone, where firedrakes render uninhabitable the burning desertlands and wyverns roost atop the barren crags of bleak mountains whose roots go down to the black abyss beneath the world. At length, after many false clues and wasted months, hope had come to him: only two months past, in the closing days of springtime, he had come upon an ancient map of the southlands below Sarkovy. He had found it in the ruins of an abandoned monastery in the mountain country, north of the Arul Pass, many leagues from the place where he had rescued the Princess Carthalla from her abductors. Once, the moldering ruins had housed a hundred monks of the Brotherhood of Light, the priestly equivalent of his own sorcerous fraternity. But long since roving bands of Thungoda had come upon the monastery: the harmless and holy men they had doubtless tortured to death with the ghoulish glee their vile kind feel when bringing agony and black death to Servants of the Higher World. And the monastery itself they had ravaged, besoiling the holy books and precious documents with the dirt of their bowels, before giving the ancient structure over to the red embrace of the fire. But this map had not burned: a hand of Power had inscribed it on a sheet of pliable metal, such as men no longer knew how to fashion. The kiss of the flames had not tarnished the imperishable flexive steel, nor dimmed the ancient traceries of a long-dead hand. Thus had Kellory at last learned of the location of Yaohim's demesne.

He stood and looked at the tower.

Strange it was, builded by magic; no hand of man had taken part in its raising. It was all of one piece, like something molded out of thick heavy dark glass, or like something that had lived and grown to this shape. The organic curves of the soaring pylon were uncanny: no structure on earth that Kellory had ever seen was so shapen. It swelled and curved and tapered to a narrow spire wherein one long, pointed window looked forth on the wilderness through which they had come. Dim was that window, shadowed, like the dusty socket of an empty skull.

But even as Kellory looked, he thought he discerned something that moved within that tall, peaked window. He looked again and there was nothing there. Perhaps it had been only his imagination, or a trick of light and shadow. He comforted himself with the thought, but he was not deceived: his eye *had* caught the flicker of movement, that he knew. For a moment, Something had stood within that tall narrow window and had gazed down at them, and had passed from their view. It was a disquieting thought; perhaps he should leave the girl behind, and press forward alone to enter the shadow-haunted tower of the long-dead mage. But no: if any Guardians lurked in this cursed vale of shadow and silence, it was only from fear of his Power that they kept from the girl.

Kellory's jaw tightened. Well did he know the strange lusts of the shadowy denizens of the Invisible World; and all too well could he guess to what repulsive and degrading uses they would twist Carthalla's slim young body—and mind—and soul. No: they must go forward together, or go back. And he would not go back, not even if he knew for very certain that a dark and grisly death awaited him in that strange tall house in the vale.

So they went forward into the tower of Yaohim.

# CHAPTER 7

## DARK CITADEL

There were no gates, no door. The portal stood open and empty. They went through into a dimness and a silence greater even than that which reigned over the strange valley beyond. Kellory walked softly, the Staff of his Power in his hand, and his eyes roamed from side to side, searching every nook and corner. His ears strained for the whisper of a voice or the echo of a footfall, but there came no sound to his ears other than that which they made. And with other senses he searched as well, senses denied to the girl at his side: the tendrils of his mind reached out through the Web of the Worlds and hearkened after tremors that should disturb— ever so slightly—the intricate and interlocking balance of forces that is the Universe. He sensed, however, nothing but the smell of ancient magics, the shadow of long-gone presences, and the resonance of once-spoken Words and Names, many of which he himself would not wish to speak aloud, far less to call upon.

The first floor was completely empty. A mere featureless oval chamber unbroken by window or doorway. An unrailed stairway glided up the curve of the wall to the second story, and Kellory and the Princess ascended by it. The girl, not daring to speak aloud lest she break Kellory's concentration, marveled much at the strange, sleek, glassy substance of the walls. It was most like a ceramic, she thought: she had seen enameled vases from the kilns of far Charabys with this kind of finish…but her imagination shuddered back from contemplating how vast must have been the furnace in which this tower was fired! The flaming hell of her religion itself would not be vast enough…

On the second floor they found naught but the rubble of decayed furniture, a few shards of pottery, scattered rags of rotten cloth, and scraps of old parchment that fell to dust at a touch. These, and cobwebs thick with the dust of centuries, and nothing more.

They searched the spaces above. One story must have been the librarium of the sorcerer, for broken and collapsing shelves of some nameless scarlet wood lined the curving walls, and a few heaps of moldering trash littered the corners, among which they found verdigris-eaten clasps and bits of oddly shaped metal such as those wherewith sealed and locked books are bound. But the Book of Shadows they found not. Nor on the next story, which had once been a laboratorium of some nature, for porcelain benches and iron tables and broken crockery still lay about, surviving the corrosion and decay of centuries. Particles of glass crunched under the step of Kellory's boot. But there were no books.

When they had searched the tower from top to bottom, they returned at length to the first floor, dispirited and weary and much besmirched with dust.

"The Book must have crumbled to dust," Carthalla said, "like those we found in the librarium above."

"Not so, girl," he grunted. He felt an inward restlessness; his eyes roved about and he prowled the room from wall to wall, pacing like a caged brute.

Exasperated with his curtness, the Princess demanded: "Why 'not so'?"

"Hush: do not disturb my thoughts," he growled. "There is something that I have forgotten (or something that had been hidden from my remembrance, one or the other). Something that I should recall…it has been years since I was last in the citadel of an enchanter…but I remember well the castle of Phazdaliom, my master…what is it that I have overlooked?"

At length he shrugged and gave up. "There is something that should be here. I *know* it should be here. But, by the Nine Faces and the Hidden Face itself, I cannot bring it to mind. Curse that vile *shioggua!* In driving it down I dangerously depleted my Inward Self… I have not that acuity of mind that I must have to find the secret!"

He tried a bit more, and finally growled and spat, and turned on his heel.

"Come on! We had best be out of here before nightfall. I cannot think of the thing that eludes me, curse the foul luck!"

"Well, then perhaps you can tell me now why the Book of Shadows would not have fallen to mold and filth, while every other book in this place has done so," she demanded tartly. Her temper was not improved by his unspoken criticism of her behavior at dawn: curse the *shioggua* indeed—and curse her for daring to bathe without asking his permission first!

"Is that what's bothering you?" he barked a curt laugh. "A Grimoire—a wizard's own Book—is imbued with his own vitality, which is more than human. Every fiber of the pages thereof, every drop of ink, is filled with supermortal energy. It takes a thousand years for wind and rain to deface a carven stone; but the Grimoire of a master magician can outlive the Aeon itself."

"Thank you for the information," she said coldly. "I will forever treasure the morsels of wisdom you let fall in my presence. And when I come to stand before the throne of my father, I will tell him of your courtesy and—and—"

She broke off, staring at him. For suddenly a grin of incredulous joy spread over his features. It was the first genuine smile she had ever seen on his face, and the dark somberness of him was lightened, made warm and even human thereby. Even his grim, cold eyes of lambent emerald fire suddenly seemed those of a man and not the shining orbs of some implacable demon of revenge.

"Bless you for your temper, Carthalla," he said. And the girl flushed crimson although she did not really know why: it was the first time he had ever called her by her name, and there was warmth in his voice.

"What—?"

"You said your father's *throne;* of course, your father has a throne, a Seat of Power, for he is a mighty Prince. But a magician is princely, too. How said my old master once? 'A wizard is a king of nature,' those were his words. And well do I remember my master seated on his chair of green crystal atop the dais of nine steps: enthroned in his Seat of Power, the magician rules the forces of the Invisible. *But where, in all this tower, is Yaohim's Seat?"*

# CHAPTER 8

## THE WHISPERING SHADOW

It took Kellory the better part of an hour to find the secret door. No ordinary man could have found the invisible crack that sundered the smooth fabric of the tower's base: but Kellory could search the molecular structure of the substance with the inner Eye of a Warlock and find that which was hidden to men. And once found, it was no great matter to gain entry. The utterance of a Word sufficed, albeit a Word that human throat and mouth were never shaped to speak.

But he had a clue that greatly eased his search: since all the tower was empty above, the throne-room of the Master Magician must lie below ground. And thus it was.

As the sound of the Word died in eerie echoes, a vast square of the floor lifted, revealing a dark yawning abyss. Up from the mouth of darkness beat a slow pulse of dim uncolored light. By this throbbing illumination, the Warlock and the Princess could dimly perceive a flight of glassy steps that descended into the maw of pallid-litten blackness.

Down the stairs they went, Kellory in the lead. He held the great black Staff of his Power before him to ward off whatever ghostly guardians the long-dead archimage might have set to watch over his magical treasures. But they descended to the dim floor of the subterranean hall without trouble.

The room was huge and long and filled with darkness. Dim shapes loomed about them in the gloom, and Kellory feared lest a careless step precipitate them into a man-trap of some kind. So he spake a Word and a dull sphere of luminance gathered out of nothingness and floated above his left shoulder, steadily growing brighter. Waves of light pulsed from it, driving back the darkness. It was a small task to sustain the Witchlight in this plane of being, and Kellory did not begrudge the slight effort—although every such work of magic took its toll on his remaining strength.

By the cold phosphorescent fire of the Witchlight they could now observe a mighty throne that stood at the far end of the room. It rested atop a huge cube of black glistening glass or crystal. When they stepped closer to observe it more carefully, Kellory saw that the upmost surface of the cube bore markings. Into the substance of the dark, glittering stuff had been inset talismans of great potency—the Seals of the Two Polarities, the Sigils of the Three Worlds, the Signs of the Four Elements, and the Signets of the Five Divinities of Darkness. Woven about these talismans, encompassing them all, was a strip of shining metal in the shape of the Quadridecagram—the Fourteen-Pointed Star.

In the center of this star stood the wizard's Throne of Power: a huge, ancient chair of black wood, carven with leering masks and devilish faces and queer glyphs. Enthroned therein, his Staff in his hand, within reach of the great talismans, Yaohim had once sat in the midst of his Power. But that was centuries ago.

About the foot of the dark, glistening cube rose small squat pedestals of stone. These bore the consecrated Instruments of the Magical Art—the Burin, the Arthame, the Bolline and the Arctrave, the stone called Ematille, the Cruse and Aspergillus, the Speculum, the Annulus, and others. Despite the tension of the moment, Kellory stared at them with admiration. They were superbly made, and beautifully crafted by a master hand. Each instrument represented many years of patient labor. To make the Arthame alone, as the Wizard's Knife was called, took seven years. Never had he seen such perfect craftsmanship!

The waxing and waning light came from the mighty Staff of Yaohim, which leaned against his Place of Power. A dim halo surrounded it. The pulsations of light throbbed like a living heart.

He did not see the Book. But he noticed that one pedestal was empty. The Throne was not.

He stiffened, sucking in his breath. Beside him, the girl clutched his bare arm, as she saw it too.

A vague Shadow sat within the chair of ancient black wood. It had no shape, no form: merely a blur of darkness, but in that darkness burned twin sparks of crimson fire like the eyes of jungle beasts.

As they watched, frozen, the Shadow darkened…thickened…gathering substance unto itself. The flaming eyes burned more fiercely now, like crimson stars.

Now, with his subtle senses, Kellory grew conscious of a Presence of Power. Power streamed from that shadow-shape, and Power was centered therein. Vast, terrific Power, with illimitable depths and strengths.

And the Shadow…*whispered!*

At first he could not make out words. Naught but a faint susurration like an uneasy wind prowling through dead dry leaves. But even as the Shadow took on shape and substance, so too did its whispering voice grow stronger. Now he could hear it plain.

*"Unwise wast thou, Warlock, to intrude upon mine slumbers."*

The Shadow spake in the Old Tongue, that is used only by wizards, priests and kings. Summoning his courage, Kellory replied in the same Tongue:

"Thou art the shade of Yaohim?"

The Shadow laughed faintly. *"I am he! Aye and verily, I that once was Lord of the Shadows am become but a Shadow myself. Thus, with such ironies, doth Fate play with the spirits of the dead!"*

The Shadow had taken full form by now. It wore the likeness of an aged man, tall and gaunt, and wrapped in tattered robes like the cerements of the grave. A tangled mane of snowy witchlocks flowed about the skull-like head of the apparition, floating on an unfelt wind. Within deep, enshadowed sockets, eyes burnt red and blazing.

And the Staff was held now in the hand of the Shadow.

"Wrongly didst thou seek to plunder mine sepulcher of its treasures, Warlock. For I shall smite thee with mine wrath and bear thee down into the Kingdom of Darkness... "

Before Kellory could move or speak, the Shadow pointed its Staff at him and uttered a potent syllable. A cold force closed about his body: a constriction that gripped and held him helpless as in a vise. By his side, the girl voiced an involuntary cry of fear as the cold uncanny force enclosed her, as well.

Kellory knew this spell; it was called the Curse of Chains. His spirits sank within him and he tasted the bitterness of despair. If he could have moved, his head would have sunken on his chest; he faltered and his courage sagged. *Alas!* he thought, *that it should come to a trial of strength: and I am already weary...*

But there was but one thing to do, and Kellory did it. He released his spirit-self from its housing of flesh and sank into the World of Darkness.

# CHAPTER 9

## BATTLE IN THE HALFWORLD

Only once before, during his training under the Green Enchanter, had Kellory ventured into the shadowy realm. And then was he fresh and well-prepared. Now, still inwardly exhausted from his great struggle with the *shioggua,* and feeling the strain of the several times he had been forced to use his Power since entering the Valley of Silence, he was in no fit condition to duel between the planes of being.

His body left behind on the physical plane, the First World, he ventured into the Dubious Land as a shape of light. This peculiar region, which lay between the world of living men and the Other World where the spirits of the dead dwell, together with certain Beings that were never alive, was not real and true. Here illusion reigned, and here all things were but symbols and representations of True Realities.

So he passed through a dim gray forest where no birds sang and naught moved or lived. The ground underfoot was a level plain, colorless as ashes, and the trees were unnaturally symmetrical. When he looked closely at them he could see they were not trees at all: but when looked at obliquely, or in passing, they seemed like enough to trees.

There were circular holes in the ashen floor: perfect circles, pits of blackness. He knew all too well what creatures sometimes dwelt in the Under Pits, and he avoided them with great care.

There was no sky overhead; no vast unending vault above the trees. The air was thick as if with mist, and the mist thickened above the tree-tops until the sight could probe no further. It was just as well. His sanity might have been endangered had he looked beyond that curtain of mist to the sky wherein black stars burned like titanic eyes.

He knew the Shadow of Yaohim would sense his flight and follow him into the Halfworld. And, ere long—as time is measured in a region that exists out of time—a shadow-shape stepped from the gray trees to confront him.

The shape of light that was the astral body of Kellory, and which went armed with a shaft of lightning brilliance that was the symboling of his Warlock's Staff in this realm of mystery, stood facing the astral self of Yaohim.

In the Halfworld, Yaohim was still a shadow. But now he stood as a towering mass of utter blackness, and his Staff was a rod of ultimate darkness.

They did not speak, for here no speech was possible. But here they could fight—and fight they did!

The rod of darkness swung to strike him, and Kellory parried it, lifting the shaft of brilliance just in time. The shock of the blow, which was not a physical impact, shook him to the core of his being. But he fought on, knowing he would never be stronger than he was now, and that with every timeless moment that passed his strength would ebb away. *Best to battle at the beginning,* he thought. But he had few hopes of surviving that battle.

The shaft of light and the rod of utter darkness flickered in an eerie dueling. Then the Shadow struck the glowing shaft aside and closed with the shape of light.

Wings of darkness enfolded the dazzling shape that was the astral self of Kellory. He struck out, a cloud of blazing splendor, coiling about the dark thing that opposed him. His shimmering tendrils sank into the darkness, and the darkness drank them in, and stifled their radiance.

Now the webs of shadow encircled Kellory and his glory dimmed, as if the darkness sought to bury and extinguish the light. Rather than struggle futilely against the slithering shadowy coils, Kellory permitted himself to be drawn into the smothering embrace of the ebon cloud. For a plan had come to him—a desperate scheme, born of desperation.

He felt his fires dim. Black, stifling veils of coldness closed about him. He was lost in the depths of an utter darkness and a terrific cold such as reigns unchallenged in the black spaces between the stars.

Even as his Power failed, half-fainting, he struck to the core of the Shadow—and seized it.

Like a black flame it burned, the Dark Star that was the inmost being of Yaohim. Every man has three bodies, Kellory knew. The first body is the physical; within that, as within a shell of flesh, lies the astral; and within that, like a Star of eternal fire, the etheric. Each body has its place and being on each of the Three Worlds. And now Kellory, with all his waning strength, seized upon the etheric Star of Yaohim and caught it within his shape of light.

The Dark Star writhed within his grasp, but he held It nonetheless. And now bright tendrils probed into the central fires, seizing upon the *chakras,* the etheric organs that are the centers of Power. One by one he mastered them.

The shadow-shape dissolved in drifting patches of umbra. The Dark Flame burned and slithered in Kellory's grasp, but he held it fast and probed within. He was greatly weakened—more than two thirds of his strength was gone. Where he had been a shape of splendor, now he was a fog-wraith of dimming light. Soon—*soon*—he must return to the First World, or drift here in the Halfworld forever, a ghost of light.

Exhausted, he released the Dark Star and it fled.

With the very dregs of his Power, he made the return passage between the worlds.

And fell limp and cold as a dead thing at the feet of Carthalla.

# CHAPTER 10

## THE QUEST GOES ON

There were times when he perceived a girl's face bending above him and heard, faint and far-off, a voice calling his name. But then the light would die in a wash of shadows and the voice would fade from his hearing.

And then, a long while later, he became conscious of sunshine. He was lying, pillowed on leaves, in the brilliance of open day. Birds were twittering and the scent of grass and flowers came to him. He felt very weary, but he felt—whole.

She came to him, there in the wizard's garden behind the tower of Yaohim, and gave him fresh water to drink, and fruit. He was content to rest and to take food from her hands, without words. He could see well enough what had happened.

The tower rose beyond him. Already its shining surface was pitted and veined with black jagged cracks. And the luster of the shimmering stuff whereof it was composed had dimmed.

Birds sang again in the woods of the Valley of Silence. And, after a while, he slept.

Day followed day and night followed night. They were comfortable enough in the shelter of the crumbling tower. Silence and shadows ruled therein no longer; neither did the undying Shadow of Yaohim dwell forever on its Throne of Power. For in conquering the master magician in that nightmare world between Life and Death, he had banished it forever from the world of men.

"It began almost at once—just after you collapsed and the Shadow was gone from the chair," Carthalla said. "I thought you were dead. The invisible bonds no longer held me and I fled up the stairs and out into the valley. And it was no longer a dead place! The boughs tossed in the wind, birds sang and fluttered, and there were small things scuttling through the grass. So I took courage and went back and found you breathing."

"How long have you tended me like this?" he asked.

"I am not sure. It was a week before you opened your eyes, and weeks more before you spoke to me. The better part of a month, I guess. You are better now?"

"Day by day my strength grows. Soon I will be able to stand. And then"—his face was dark and there was bitterness in the grim set of his jaw—"then I must go on again."

"Whither?"

"South; into the desert country," he muttered. "For at the last, as I probed into the centers of his being, I read that Yaohim had given over the Book of Shadows into the hands of his disciple, Pnomphet, a sorcerer who dwells in Ashangabar, the Dead City. There must I quest still, in search of the Book of Shadows." There was dark defeat and great weariness in his eyes and he stared broodingly towards the mountains of the South.

The girl, who sat near him, the grimy rags of her gown scarce covering her beauty, looked down at him and said, softly:

"I will go with you…"

Her face was very close to his. But he made no answer, merely looking up at her from the sterile depths of his bitterness. He had never known the love of woman, and never thought to do so. For his name was Vengeance, and Vengeance was his god.

But he stared, and hoped he could always remember the exact, exquisite color of her soft limpid eyes…no matter how the Quest ended thereafter.

# PART 3

## THE CITY WHERE DEATH WAS KING

# CHAPTER 1

## THE BLACK WOLF

An hour before sunfall they had reached the foot of the narrow pass across the Mandragon Mountains, and here they made camp. The tall, lean man with the somber face and the unearthly green eyes selected a pocket in the foothills ringed about with boulders for their encampment. He liked being able to set his back against a wall of solid stone. His name was Kellory.

The girl, Carthalla, unpacked the saddlebags the three horned and shaggy little ponies had carried across the mountains. These restive, unruly, half-wild beasts they had taken from the Thungoda war party Kellory had ambushed and slain with his witchfire many weeks before. As she unrolled the sleeping furs and set out their meager repast of dried fruit, salted meat, black bread and sour red wine, she grimaced wryly: reared a Princess of the Blood in the silken palaces of Grand Khev to the north, she never dreamed to find herself toiling like a slave-woman. But here she was, grimy with road-dust, her golden hair greasy and disheveled, her hands callused and black with ground-in dirt.

She glanced across the little open space at the man who had saved her from the Thungoda—the man she had perforce accompanied this far on his quest for an old book of spells. What a grim, cold, silent man he was, she thought bitterly to herself; while the blood in his veins might be as royal as her own, and even more ancient, he was not even a warrior, much less a noble: naught but a wandering adventurer with a crippled right hand and the tall black Staff of an enchanter; a somber, grim, brooding man given to few words and no laughter.

Carthalla found him depressing company. She was even a little afraid of him, in a way, although he had never touched her and seemed not to realize that she was a woman. This alone would have been sufficient cause to pique her curiosity, were it not that she knew him to be obsessed with his mission of vengeance against the Thungoda, a path which he had sternly followed throughout his life and from which he would never deviate.

Just now, the man called Kellory was squatting on his heels, regarding a shallow hole which he had scooped in the sandy soil and filled with dry gorse and heather and the broken branches of a dead tree. He was staring thoughtfully down at the pile of brush: in repose, his lean, dark face was gaunt and impassive, almost handsome in a way (she thought, with a little catch in her heart). He did not wear his hair in the thick braid of a warrior, but let it hang about his features in tangled witchlocks. Under scowling black brows his eyes brooded, weirdly green; and his thin, pinched lips were held tight, like a half-healed wound.

Carthalla shivered. The men she had known all her seventeen years, young, laughing knights and gay courtiers, had been golden-haired and fair of complexion, with smiling blue eyes—very unlike this hard, grim wolf of a Warlock! During the weeks they had ridden together he had spoke but seldom, and then to the point. He had kept much to himself, riding off into the hills to hunt, keeping his thoughts and his emotions unspoken.

And he had never even touched her! Carthalla pursed her full soft lips in a little pout: it was not that she wished to lose her maidenhead to this dark, strange man from the cold wastes of the North—not at all! She certainly did not desire him; she didn't even like him. But the men she had known at court made of love a game: she was used to adroitly fending off flirtatious gallantries, and she expected such.

But it was not Kellory's way. Half of the time, she could almost swear, he was thoroughly unaware that she existed. Hour after hour he would sit, hunched in the saddle, brooding on his cold, savage dreams of vengeance, oblivious to the loveliness of the half-naked girl who went with him, unwillingly, but unable to resist his will.

She had never seen or heard of a man like Kellory, had Carthalla, and in an odd, indefinable way he fascinated her. Still, she wished he would talk more, and tell her of his strange boyhood on the plains of the North, among the Black Wolf nation, his tribe, and of the long war his people had waged alone against the horde of the Thungoda, who had come drifting down into these parts of the world from the unknown fastnesses of the Ultimate North, to loot and ravage and destroy. He was the last of his people, she knew, was Kellory the Black Wolf. And he lived only to avenge their destruction…

A sudden flare of green light made her start and cry out involuntarily. Kellory had not struck steel against flint to ignite the fire that now blazed up, crackling through the mounded brush. He had only laid his left hand upon the heap—the hand which wore, on its middle finger, a narrow iron ring graven with a single glyph in no tongue yet spoken by men upon all this world of Zephrondus—and uttered a Word (harsh, clanging, heavy with consonants), and the flames had sprung into being! Flames, she noticed, with a little shiver, green as the depths of his somber eyes.

Carthalla moved her shoulders a little in distaste. Magicians she had known before, for the Seven Cities of Sarkovy were filled with them. But, for the most part, they had been fat and comfortable and glib of tongue. They had not prepared her for the experience of a man like Kellory... As she watched, he rose lithely, went to tend their shaggy ponies, leaving it to the Crown Princess of Grand Khev to make ready their repast.

Her lips tightened as she bent to the task.

No; she did not even like the man she had accompanied into the deserts of the South.

# CHAPTER 2

## KNIVES IN THE NIGHT

Other eyes had glimpsed that uncanny flash of green flame as well as had Carthalla's. High on the crags that leaned like stony shelves from the cliffs of the mountains, dark riders with eyes like hawks had seen the flare of unexpected light where no light should be. Now, dismounting, they crept to the brink of the crag and peered down.

Above, the sun-star Kylix, now sinking into the west in a sea of scarlet flame, painted the upper parts of the mountains with fierce gold. Below, the foothills were drowned in purple shadows. But the eyes of the Riders of Khun were keen as the hunting-hawks they were named after, and soon they had searched out the figure of the tall cloaked man in black leather and the slender, golden girl.

And the three ponies! Hawk-like eyes narrowed craftily. This pass over the mountains was known as the Vale of Khoth, and it was used by very many merchants. Generally, the trader-caravans went heavily guarded, but more than one clever tradesman of Sarkovy had sought to slip through the pass with a smaller party. And, also generally, that had meant gems…

With a few muttered words, the desert warriors remounted and guided their sure-footed ponies down the crags, from level to level, by roads known only to such as they.

* * * *

Having eaten and drunk lightly, now wrapped in his warm cloak, Kellory sat with his back against a boulder, his fathomless gaze staring out into the moonlit wastes of the desert. Tomorrow, with dawn, they must attempt that sea of sand, for somewhere within it lay whatever morsels Time had left ungnawed of the Dead City of Ashangabar, once the home of the prophet Pnomphet, and the repository of his wisdom. It was not a journey which Kellory wished to make, for the deserts of the South were strange to him, and he preferred the wild and wintry plains and mountains of the North, where his heart was at home. But the quest which drove him mercilessly must be pursued, and there was little room in him for aught else. Sometimes he wished it were not so; at other times he felt a fierce and lonely pride in the destiny which was his alone.

The girl came and knelt by his side; as was usual with him, Kellory ignored her presence. She looked out at the moonlight which lay on the soft sands like silver dust on the folds of a piece of silk.

"It is very beautiful, by night," she said dreamily.

Kellory's pale lips twisted in a savage smile. There was no mirth in it, that smile.

"It is somewhat less beautiful by day," he said. "Death dwells in those dunes, and a terrible death it is. The death of thirst, the death of the burning sun…"

"And are you afraid of death?" she asked, almost challengingly.

His somber expression did not change, but something flickered within his strange eyes.

"Once my quest is done and the Thungoda have gone down to grovel before the Black Throne of Pnom," he said tonelessly, "I will embrace Death as a lover his bride. For life will hold no longer anything for me…"

"That is a sad, and a foolish, thing to say!" the girl cried indignantly. Kellory said nothing, his face tightening. The girl swore under her breath, and tried to change the subject.

"Do you think we will find the Book of Shadows in the ruins of Ashangabar?" she asked. The dark man shrugged.

"Once it was the residence of Pnomphet," he said. "Since we did not discover the Grimoire in the tower of Yaohim, mayhap he bequeathed it into the hands of the foremost of his disciples. But these things happened, all of them, long ago. That which I read in the heart of Yaohim, what time I wrestled with him in the Halfworld, led me to believe that the prophet held the Book, for a time, at least…"

"What if the Book no longer exists?" asked Carthalla.

Kellory made no answer to that question.

It is difficult to hold a conversation with a naked sword at your throat.

# CHAPTER 3

## THE HAWKS OF KHUN

The grinning men in their long striped *allats* had materialized out of the darkness like spirits summoned by a conjurer. One moment the shadows between the rocks were empty: the next, and they were filled with robed men and naked steel. Carthalla squeaked and shrank into the curve of Kellory's arm. As for Kellory, he said nothing, neither did a muscle so much as move in his face. He regarded them with thoughtful eyes.

"Here is no fat-gutted merchant of Sarkovy," growled the leader of the desert men, looking disappointed. "Ahd—search the saddlebags!"

This was done, quickly enough, and, of course, there was nothing. "No gems at all, my chieftain," muttered Ahd. "Not even so much as a single pearl!"

Stroking his dark red beard with one lean, swarthy hand, his eyes narrowing as they searched the slim long legs and high breasts of the blond girl, the chieftain of the raiders smiled.

"Here, at very least, is a pearl among women," he observed. "And a golden pearl, at that!" Carthalla flushed and dropped her eyes, unwilling to meet the eyes that gloated upon her naked flesh, generously exposed to view in the rents of her tattered gown.

"The woman is not for you, wolf of the desert," said Kellory without inflection.

"Nor for the likes of you, wolf of the steppes," returned the other. At his command they pulled Kellory to his feet. He stood, regarding them with cold, level eyes, arms folded upon the black leather of his tunic. His great, iron-shod Staff lay still propped against the boulder near to hand, but to Carthalla's surprise he did not attempt to seize it.

The desert chief looked him over curiously. "I know you for a man of the North," he said after a time, "for I have seen the men of Barbaria before—in the slave marts of Novodny! But never before have I seen a man like you…you are no warrior, for you have not the plaited hair of the warriors of the North. But you bear yourself like one. Wolf of the Cold Wastes, what manner of man are you?"

Kellory said nothing.

After a time, they searched him, finding a few coins in his purse and a cluster of talismans worn about his throat on a cord under his tunic. The talismans were of iron, scarlet stone, white paste: of no value to the desert men, although many a magician there was in the world whose eyes would have lit with delight and cupidity, could he have glimpsed them.

"What has happened to your hand?" demanded the chieftain, for the right hand of Kellory—the hand that holds a sword—was stiff and inflexible, cased in a glove of hard black leather.

"They held it in the fires until it was dead," said Kellory tonelessly. Stripping off the glove, the desert men saw that this was so. Carthalla paled and averted her eyes from the burnt lump of scar-tissue; and more than a few of the desert men looked away, muttering an oath under their breaths. Without speaking, Kellory freed his arms from the grasp of those that held him, and covered the crippled hand in its old casing of black leather.

"Man, man, who did this thing to you?" whispered the chieftain, almost in awe.

"The Thungoda of the North," said Kellory.

The chieftain looked away, studying the remnants of the meal, the embers of the fire, the long Staff, the tethered ponies munching their grain.

"You bear nothing of worth. You do not even go armed. And you are a man of the North. What seek you here in the deserts of the South?"

"I seek vengeance for that which was done to me and for the death of my nation."

"Vengeance? How?"

Kellory smiled a thin, wintry smile. "Through an old book," he said idly. The chieftain swore, spat and threw up his hands.

"Here is a riddle beyond my wit!" he exclaimed. "Hawks of Khun, let us bear these two and their gear into the camp of Khun our lord, that he may unriddle the mystery."

Ahd grunted and tugged at his pointed beard.

"'Twere wiser we cut down the man and sold the woman in the marts of Novodny," he grumbled. "Such would I do, were *I* chieftain, like unto Shamad."

"The wits of Ahd are thick and heavy," said the chieftain, grinning. "This is the reason why Shamad is leader here, and Ahd but follows. Lord Khun will search out the secret, never fear."

They mounted up and rode into the sandy waste, with Kellory and Carthalla their prisoners.

# CHAPTER 4

## KHUN OF THE NINE SKULLS

There were ten of the desert men. As they rode, they made an open box-like formation, with Kellory and Carthalla, on their ponies with the pack-beast galloping along behind, in the center of the hollow square. It was, Carthalla soon discovered, uncomfortable to ride with your wrists lashed before you to the saddle horn and your ankles roped together under the belly of your mount.

As they rode into the desert, Carthalla stole sidewise glances at Kellory's immobile features. He did not deign to turn his head and meet her glance. The girl was frightened; but she was also rather exasperated at the passivity of her companion. Once she had watched him slay nine Thungoda warriors in three heartbeats: his witchfire had smote them from the saddles like bolts of lightning. They had been dead before they had time enough to scream. Why, then, did he hold back from striking down the desert men?

His behavior was a puzzle to her. But, then, almost everything about the lone adventurer puzzled her.

As for Kellory, his keen eyes missed nothing. Not the brace of hill-fowl bound to each saddle, which told him as well as did the long black bows across their shoulders that this was a hunting-party. Nor the direction in which they were riding. Nor the fact that the desert men had flung aside his iron-shod Staff, deeming it worthless. Without his blasting wand, Kellory's powers were limited. But there was nothing he could do about it.

They rode into the encampment, finding it a double circle of capacious tents of felt dyed scarlet, erected against the shelter of a curve of rocky hills. In the center of the double circle rose one tent larger than the rest: tassels of braided gold wire swung from the fringes of the tent-flap, and planted deep in the sand before the entrance thereto was a tall standard of carved and ancient wood with three cross-braces. Bound to pegs upon the cross-pieces were the skulls of nine monsters. Kellory did not at once recognize the beasts from which the prizes had been taken.

Shamad led his troop up before the tent of his lord with a flourish, and flung himself from the saddle, tossing the reins to a servant. Ahd and the others hauled Kellory and the girl roughly down, slashing their bonds with hooked knives. They were led within.

On a nest of plump cushions, smoking a long, long pipe of carved crimson wood sat a remarkably ugly man.

He was thin as a starving child, with cheekbones that jutted from his long-jawed face, casting deep hollow shadows down his sunken cheeks from the light of many fat, perfumed candles. He had gentle, wise, soft eyes that twinkled with mischief and good humor, under grotesquely tufted brows. Grotesque, as well, was his enormous beak of a nose, and the sweep of stiff gray mustachios (glistening with wax) which curved like sickles to either side of his face. His head was covered with silken scarves wound and knotted into a turban-like arrangement. He wore pantaloons of gaudy fabric, sewn with seed-pearls, a huge sash of canary yellow, into which were thrust three long knives, and boots of purple Kavlad leather, with toes that curled up, and from the toes hung tiny gold bells. Gold bells hung in his earlobes as well, and from the bristling tips of his greased mustachios.

"Whom have you brought before me, Shamad, you offspring of a toad and a lizard, with half the wits of either?" the curious old man inquired in a tender, sweet voice. Shamad stood very tall, and smote his left breast with the balled fist of his right hand. In a rapid, breathless voice, he related the events which had recently occurred. He did not meet the gentle, humorous gaze of his lord as he made his report, but stared at an imaginary point in midair above his chief's turbaned head.

Kellory noticed that the leader of the huntsmen stammered just a little in his speech; also, that perspiration glittered on his swarthy brow. From this, and from his ability to read men, he guessed that the sweet-voiced old man with the clown's face and huge nose was very dangerous, or very unpredictable. Or both.

"And what account do you give of yourself, stranger from the steppes?" inquired Khun softly, when Shamad had finished. Kellory met the gaze of the desert lord squarely, but without provocation; there was nothing to be gained from showing fear or belligerence. Such as Khun would not be impressed by either.

"I am called Kellory," he said quietly. "My tribe is the Black Wolf nation of the North. In Barbaria was I born. From Barbaria was I driven by the Thungoda, who drift down out of the Ultimate North in their tens of thousands."

"Was it the Thungoda did *that* to you," murmured Khun, nodding at his crippled hand, "or were you punished for thievery or murther by your fellow tribesmen?"

In a voice cold and hard and brittle as a steel blade in winter, Kellory related as much of his story as he cared Khun to know. The old man nodded thoughtfully, puffing on his long crimson pipe.

"We have heard of these Thungoda, even we," said Khun when Kellory had finished. "And what do you here in the Sea of Sand?"

"To avenge my murdered people, I became a Warlock. Since I could not fight my enemies with the sword, I vowed to fight them with sorcery. My youth I devoted to the study of the Nine Arts. I entered into the Brotherhood of Darkness. I learned of a mighty magician of a time earlier than our own: Yaohim, they called him, which in the Old Tongue means Lord of Shadows. He alone possessed mastery of a strange, forgotten lore by which he destroyed the Sea Devils in all their many thousands. This secret he wrote into a book: I am here in search of the Book."

Khun regarded the tall man, shrewd eyes measuring him from head to foot. He did not for one moment believe Kellory's tale. Vengeance he understood, for the desert tribes were rife with blood feud and vendetta. What he did not believe was that Kellory sought a book. Like most of his tribe, Khun was unable to read or write, and men tend to depreciate that which is beyond them.

Khun tapped out his pipe in a little bowl of hammered brass.

"It is nearly the hour of Prayer: we will talk again of these matters, Wolf of the North," he said sweetly. "Jazool, conduct these twain to the Tent of Knives. See that they have food and drink, if they desire them, and bedding. See to it that they are closely guarded, for wizards are a chancy folk."

As they were led forth from the red tent, Kellory passed the standard of the nine monster-skulls. Now he recognized them, and a chill of unease touched his spine.

They were the skulls of mandragons.

# CHAPTER 5

## ACROSS THE SEA OF SAND

Kellory accepted a flask of wine, and bade Carthalla do the same, for nights on the Sea of Sand were cold, he had heard. The girl was exasperated with him, and teeming with questions; as soon as they were alone, she let them out.

"Why did you not smite them with your witchfire when they seized us, as you smote the Thungoda?" she demanded hotly.

He looked at her with cold, indifferent eyes. "Less than two moons have passed since I fought the shade of Yaohim in the Dubious Land beyond the world," he said briefly. "You will remember how close to death I was, and how you nursed me back to strength. The strength of my body has been restored, but within me, my Power is still weak, for much was drained from me in that struggle."

"You lit the bonfire with a Word," she countered, "as I have seen you do before." He nodded, witchlocks stirring.

"A test, to see if I could still do it. And I would that I had refrained, for doubtless it was that flash of green fire in the gloom that caught the eyes of the Hawks of Khun."

"What do you think he will do with us?" she murmured, settling into her bedroll. He shrugged.

"Slay me, and sell you in the slave mart," he said. "If he is wise. But Khun measures all men by himself, which is not wise. He does not believe me about the Book. He suspects that we search for the Dead City after treasure, for that is a motive such men as Khun understand. We shall have to wait and see...and wait for my Power to renew itself."

"What can you do without your Staff?" she whispered listlessly.

Kellory smiled a thin smile, saying nothing.

\* \* \* \*

It eventuated that Kellory had been accurate in his estimate of Khun. For on the morrow they were bidden again to the great tent of the Nine Skull Standard, and the bony little old man with the enormous nose blandly announced that he was willing to escort Kellory and the girl to the Dead City with all his host of warriors. Kellory accepted the offer without comment. They broke their fast and rode from the camp before the world was an hour older.

The two had donned the loose, voluminous *allats* of the desert men: with their full sleeves and cowls they shielded the body from the fierce rays of the sun-star, without blocking the breeze.

The desert country was very different from the wintry steppes of the North or the grassy plains of Sarkovy. There, at least, the ground was firm beneath your feet, but here with each step you sank into the softness of the sands. The ponies labored, floundering, and made poor time. But the tribesmen sought out rocky ridges to follow through the waste, where the desert wind had blown the sands away, and their progress improved.

Khun fell back to ride beside Kellory for a time, and the two conversed. Khun was curious about magic.

"With your Power, Warlock," he said gently, "why cannot you but call this Book to you, as your kind call up demons and spirits?"

"Were the Book of Shadows sentient, Lord of the Desert, perhaps I could. But a thing that does not live cannot hear."

Khun laughed heartily. "You have wit, Black Wolf!" he observed. "I, who rule a pack of fools, often miss the wisdom and the wit of cultured men."

"I have a question of my own," said Kellory. "Do you truly know the whereabouts of the city?" The desert chief nodded, which made the little gold bells in each lobe and the points of his mustachios tinkle sweetly.

"Ashangabar has its back set against the mountains," he said, smiling, "and faces the desert as a warrior fronts a foe. But the desert won."

"What do you mean?"

"You will see, Black Wolf," said Khun. And no longer did he smile. "You will see a city where Death is king."

Then he thumped his bootheels in the ribs of his mount and cantered forward to rejoin his chieftains, leaving Kellory alone with his brooding thoughts.

Erelong, hills rose before them, gaunt black rocks rising from the waves of red sand like shipwrecks half-drowned in surf. The city was not far off, the Warlock knew, for they were near the mountains now. They marched across the world like a row of stony giants, the mountains. Entering the rock hills, Kellory noticed that the chief dispatched outriders and that the desert warriors unlimbered their bows and spears, as if fearing the nearness of enemies.

"Is there danger in these hills?" he inquired of one of the guards who rode near them, a lank, sour-faced man called Kammud. The guard opened his mouth to make reply, but then, and suddenly, no answer was needed. For a scaly green shape rose from the fissures of the rock and caught Kammud from the saddle, fanged jaws crunching about the man's head.

# CHAPTER 6

## THE GREEN DEATH

The thing was thrice the size of a man, with hulking shoulders and long ape-like arms; vaguely anthropoid, it had, however, the hindquarters of a reptile, and the spiny tail. Reptilian, too, were the glistening green scales of its hide, the fanged jaws, the gaping nostrils. But the most horrible thing about it was its head, which resembled the head of a man, with its blunt snout and square mouth. Man-like, too, was the bristling mane of green spines it wore as men wear their hair.

Strong jaws crunched. Bone snapped, blood spurted. And Kammud went down to the Kingdom of Shadows headless.

The mandragon reached out an impossibly long arm, hooked claws clutching. Carthalla shrieked; her pony panicked, bucked, threw her prone on the sand. For a moment the man-dragon loomed above her, blinking its huge owlish eyes, slobber drooling down its scaly breast. The Hawks of Khun whirled about, and with spears leveled, tried to ride the monster down. But their javelins snapped off against the green mail.

Kellory crouched in the sand, hands open as if to grasp empty air. Globules of sweat gleamed on his brow, on his cheeks: his eyes were blank, gaze turned inwards towards the centers of Power, focusing—
*"Hither to my hand, Haklamaklan!"* he called, his voice raw and hoarse with the effort. The mandragon, crouching above the helpless girl, blinked irritably at the dark man in black leather.

Something came twinkling through the air, faster than a bird can fly. It snapped into his grasp and he rose to his full height, brandishing it before him. The desert men gaped in awe and amazement; for it was the long black wood Staff of Power they had left behind in the foothills when Kellory was captured.

The mandragon stared at him, mad eyes wide and witless, glaring like yellow moons. Those eyes were devoid of mind or soul, filled only with hatred for everything that lived. And with a bottomless hunger.

He faced the monstrous thing, the Staff held before him in both hands. His eyes were green flame and green ice, his mien stern, commanding, resolute. When he addressed the beast, each syllable of his words rang like iron gongs.

"Go from us now, mandragon! We are no food for such as you. Go back down into your black hole. Must I call upon the Timeless Ones—the Guardians of the Balance? I speak the Name PHUOL LUMNIVUUR! IOGNUGGONG! ZOAR! Go from us, Unclean Thing! I am a Warlock of the Secret Flame. My circle is the Ninth; my sphere the Sphere of Darkness; my god the Lord of Mysteries. And I hold in my hand the Keys of Power. *Go—from—us.*"

It seemed to those who watched, frozen, that the tall shape of Kellory, wrapped in his long cloak and striped *allot,* darkened like a pillar of black night. Grew tall and vast, like a tower of jet. That his eyes blazed like whirling globes of emerald supernal fire. That his words rang and echoed among the hills like growling thunder.

The world shook slightly, underfoot; the skies of noontide darkened as if with a crawling film. A wind sprang up, cold as the black wind that blows at the bottom of the world, where dead men roam forever the bleak and lonely halls of Pnom.

The monster flinched from that burning gaze. Claws as long as sickles were sheathed. It lumbered about, crawling clumsily into the dark fissure in the rock. It sank from view.

His face wet and gray, Kellory stumbled—would haves fallen, but men sprang to support him. His head hung down, sweat dripping from the ends of his hair. It had taken much of his strength, but the thing was gone and it was done.

\* \* \* \*

They buried Kammud in the sand at the place where he had died, knowing that his ghost would keep this ravine forever free of mandragons. And they rested for a time, to calm the ponies and to permit the Warlock to recover something of his strength. From a bottle of thick black glass, set with polished but uncut gems, Khun poured a cup of luscious golden brandy filched from a king's treasure.

Kellory dutifully drank it down, for it was a gesture almost of homage that the Lord of the Desert shared his private stock with his prisoner. But, when no one watched, he took from a hidden pocket in his leather garment a flat box of old silver, and imbibed two pinches of a powder made of colorless crystals like crushed glass.

The drug was dangerous, even deadly: but somehow Kellory knew that he would need all of his strength for what lay ahead.

"So that was a mandragon," he mused later. Khun nodded soberly.

"My people call them the Green Death," the old man muttered, and for once his tones were harsh. "They infest these mountains like maggots in a rotting corpse. Some whisper they are kin-murderers, oath-breakers, changed to monsters for their sins. No one knows, but they are more like men than you would think, Black Wolf: clever and cunning as serpents, terrible in battle as the great cats of the jungles to the south…"

"Your standard bears the skulls of such," Kellory murmured.

"I slew the nine with my own hand, when I was young," acknowledged Khun. "It was accounted a mighty feat. And so, perhaps, it was. But you…" He eyed Kellory's lined and weary face with a troubled, puzzled gaze. "You drove it from the maid with words alone…whereas we know, from of old, that even sharp steel is seldom enough to fright them away, much less to slay them. When we slay such, we employ deep-dug pits, lined with sharp stakes."

Kellory gave a wan and mirthless smile. It had taken far more than merely words to force the huge mandragon into flight, although it must have seemed no more than that to the desert men. It had taken an effort of will such as few men, save those steeped in the mental disciplines of wizards, could have been capable of. For a magician works his wonders by forcing his will upon nature and by bending its forces in obedience to his command. But only he knew how terribly the feat of repelling the mandragon had taxed his reserves of strength.

"I would not care to attempt it again, right now," he murmured.

"Nathless, the feat was mightier than mine own," said Khun almost humbly. Kellory made no reply.

"Here is food," said Carthalla. She knelt by the Warlock and offered a steaming bowl. He ate hungrily: the ragout was thick with good meat, rich with spiced gravy, hot and peppery. He could have eaten thrice the amount, but did not ask for more.

Khun looked around him. "Here will we make camp, that you may rest. The day is well advanced—"

Kellory shook his head, though every fiber of his body wept with fatigue.

"We go forward, Hawk of the Sands, for we must enter the City of Death before moonrise," he said. And there was iron in his voice.

Khun looked down at him without expression.

"It shall be as you wish, Wolf of the North," he said softly.

# CHAPTER 7

## A CITY LIKE A SKULL

They came to the ruins of Ashangabar an hour before sunfall and reined their steeds to a halt, and sat looking it over.

Even as Khun had told, the city was built with its back set against the black cliffs of the mountain, gates and watch-towers facing the Sea of Sand. All of red stone was Ashangabar, minarets and domes and cupolas and long shadowy arcades. From a central plaza, broad boulevards radiated outwards to the walls, like the spokes of a wagonwheel. On the far side of the plaza, rising in tiers built squarely up against the black stone of the cliff, rose the citadel of the Princes.

It was very dead, was Ashangabar. The red stone, once sleek, was worn and pitted, cracked and crumbling, scoured by fierce suns and hot, dry winds. Flake by flake the very fabric of the city was disintegrating into sand. For in their long struggle, the desert had won at last: and, like a conquering army, the red sands of the desert had poured through the open gates of Ashangabar, to drift into the streets.

Towers had fallen, and others leaned awry. Domes had broke and reared only shards against the sky. The city resembled nothing so much as a parched and broken skull, half-buried in the shifting sands. It looked as if it had died ten thousand years ago, but Kellory knew that only centuries had gone by since Ashangabar had flourished, green with gardens, sweet with fountains, rich with flowering trees.

"What killed it?" he inquired at last.

"The wise men of my people say, The Whispering Death," answered Khun shortly. "But I do not know what they mean by it."

"Let us hope we do not find out," said Kellory.

And they rode down between the open gates; and thus they came at last to Ashangabar.

\* \* \* \*

It did not take the desert tribesmen long to discover that the city was completely uninhabited by men. They searched the streets and houses, but found no trace that men had lived here in a very long time. And this made them uneasy—this, and one other thing.

For not only was Ashangabar deserted by men, it was also barren of life in any form, as dead as the cold moons that floated in the velvet skies. The wells and fountains were bone-dry; not even mold or lichen beslimed their depths and cisterns. No lizards sunned themselves on the sills or terraces. No scorpions dwelt in the ruined gardens. Even the red vipers of the desert shunned the crypts and sewers of the ruined city. Perhaps it was, as the old men said, killed by a curse.

For dead it was, dead as dead can be.

They camped that night in the central plaza, for even the desert warriors did not care to sleep within the walls of the empty, deserted houses, and the night was fair. They built huge fires of the ancient furniture found within the abandoned dwellings; these cast rich orange light and drove the night away…but, also, they cast immense, crawling black shadows over the dead walls and the black, empty windows that were like the hollow sockets in a skull.

They feasted, but Kellory observed that the men did not like this place and that, in their carousal, laughter rang hollow and the whites of their eyes showed as they started fearfully at every sound. The tribesmen of the desert were no more or no less superstitious than were the men of the Seven Cities of Sarkovy, or the warriors of his own bleak steppes, he knew. But something here frightened them, although nothing showed its face.

Perhaps, because it had no face…

He moved his shoulders irritably, as if to shrug the thought away. His mentor, Phazdaliom the Green Enchanter, had taught him much as a boy. He could read nine languages, could Kellory, and three of them were as dead as Ashangabar itself, and two of them had never been spoken by men on this planet. The myriad books in the librarium of Phazdaliom had he devoured in his hunger for knowledge and the power it gave him for revenge. Wiser and more learned than the sages of Sarkovy was the dark man—why, then, did the dead city frighten even him?

For frighten him it did. And he was no ignorant savage, to start at shadows and fear ghosts. But he sensed something old and dread here, but alive. A malignance, watchful and insatiable and beyond the reach of years…something that slept within these walls, perchance to wake only when men came near…to slay again. As the Plague sleeps in the frozen graves of wasted cities, to wake and stalk the earth with spring.

He shuddered, and grimly turned his thoughts away.

That night, the first of them went mad.

# CHAPTER 8

## WHISPERS IN THE DARK

It was a sentry called Hamood. They found him at the end of his shift. He lay curled in a ball like a frightened child, whimpering and slobbering, his face empty and his eyes wide and dull, as if the mind behind them was dead. Carthalla pressed white knuckles against her teeth, clutching Kellory's arm. Kellory said nothing, but his dark face was cold and hard as iron.

"He keeps muttering the same thing over and over again," Shamad hissed between clenched teeth. "'Stop the Whispers,' he says. 'Make the Whispers stop'—'tis uncanny. What think you, Warlock?"

"I think the wise men of your tribe were right when they said the city was slain by The Whispering Death," said Kellory briefly. Turning on his heel, he stalked away to stare at the empty houses, the broken walls. Somewhere behind them Something lurked, and watched, and waited. Something he could not see, but whose presence he felt in every fiber of his being.

He hefted the iron-shod Staff, taking thin comfort from the smooth wood and heavy weight of Haklamaklan.

\* \* \* \*

Khun mounted two sentries at every post and let the rest of the men sleep. But it was an uneasy slumber they found that night, tossing and turning restlessly, a slumber heavy with bad dreams.

Khun and Kellory prowled from guardpost to guardpost, but naught occurred the remainder of that night. Although the sentries did report hearing whispers from the shadows, whispers too faint for their ears to make out the words, however they strained. Khun dismissed these tales as idle foolishness; Kellory was not so certain.

"The wind prowls through these empty buildings, and the driftsand hisses beneath its passage," scoffed Khun. "'Tis that they hear, not the whispering of ghosts—and a whisper cannot kill or harm."

"Tell that to Hamood," said the Warlock moodily.

He wondered where in all this wilderness of standing stone and rubble had the prophet Pnomphet made his home. Khun had heard of this prophet, for the men of the desert place much credence in soothsayers and fortune-tellers, and holy men who bear to earth messages from the gods. But it was only legends Khun had to tell.

"They drave him forth from the city for some impiety, men say, or for some prophecy that went wrong or did not come to pass," said Khun.

"Into the desert?"

The old desert chief nodded. "Into the desert to die of thirst or of the sun. Tis a hard way to perish…"

"No worse than being driven mad by whispers," commented the Warlock. "Think you that his tomb lies outside the city, somewhere in the waste?"

Khun shrugged and spat. "They say his disciples accompanied him to the slow death of exile. If that be true, then there were hands to rear a tomb for him, unless your prophet was the last to die."

"We will search the city first," decided Kellory. "Pnomphet might not have had a chance to bear the Book of Shadows with him."

The old chief grinned craftily, a twinkle in his mild, gentle eyes. He was still skeptical of Kellory's legendary Grimoire, believing that it would require something of greater value than scribbled pages to lure the Black Wolf into this place, leaving the lush meadowlands of Sarkovy behind. But he was beginning to feel respect and affection for the somber, silent man who had driven down the mandragon. He was not sure: but he was patient enough to wait and see. And if there was treasure, well, his men were many…

Kellory smiled inwardly, for he could almost read the thoughts of the chief. Not that it mattered greatly to him what Khun thought or believed.

With dawn, as Kylix rose over the eastern desert, they found another madman. He had been unable to slumber, had he, and lay awake for hours staring into the shadows, straining his ears to hear the words whose import he could never quite make out. When the chieftains roused their men at sunrise, they found him hopelessly mad, giggling to himself as he tried to stuff his fingers into ears already mangled and bloody from his nails and the rings he wore.

Khun groaned a curse, tugging savagely on his mustachios. He began to wish he had never set eyes on this Warlock, or heard of his fool's quest.

The desert men do not venerate the mad, but exterminate them swiftly. They slit the throats of the two and buried them in the earth, prising up the slabs of pavement to dig their graves. Carthalla thought it was barbaric: her people embalmed their dead, and buried them in tombs of clean marble. Ever Kellory did not approve: his folk burnt their fallen on great fires, that their spirits might ascend to their fathers. But to every people their own customs.

* * * *

After the morning meal, the tribesmen were anxious to begone from this accursed place where naught lived but unseen voices in the night. Khun, however, was made of stronger mettle. If the evanished princes had left a golden hoard somewhere in the ruins of Ashangabar, he meant to have it. Yet even he felt dubious and fretful.

"Long ago, we searched this place, finding naught of value save worn old tapestries and a few lamps of pierced silver," he told Kellory. "In the days of our fathers, scattered gems and carvings of jade and of lapis were plundered here. But always the shadows and the whispers drave our people hence. Surely, Wolf, there is nothing here of worth or we would have found it, long ago."

"Nothing that you would prize, perchance," said Kellory. "For the Hawks of Khun neither read nor write, and despise such city-ways as vain frivolities, is it not true? But the Book has value to me, at least. Give me this day and another night."

Khun scratched the tip of his long nose with a gilded fingernail, looking unhappy. But to return to the encampment of the tribe would be admitting himself capable of error, and he would lose face; and many were the younger, stronger warriors who already eyed his position hungrily.

"Very well; another night, then," he grumbled, strolling off.

"What can we find, in that small time?" sighed Carthalla.

"The home of Death," said Kellory somberly.

# CHAPTER 9

## SOMETHING IN THE SHADOWS

All that long day, the tribesmen searched the abandoned ruins of the city, turning up a few meager trinkets, but nothing of greater worth than the hilt of an old, rusted sword, set with opals. Khun snarled at them when they brought it to him.

"Am I a pack rat, to gloat over such trash!" he raged, slapping the men across the face. They fell on their bellies and let him beat them till he wearied. Kellory said nothing: the Lord of the Desert was feared for his savage temper, his murderous wrath, he gathered. It would be unwise to incur the ire of Khun.

The day dragged on interminably. Men measured the lengthening shadows with eager eyes, impatient to be gone. *One more night*, their lord had vowed…*and how many of them, with dawn, would still be sane?* They muttered darkly amongst themselves, stroking hooked knives with horny thumbs, eyeing Khun when they did not think he was watching.

He was watching, of course; Khun had not held mastery over this band of desert bandits for these many years without developing eyes in the back of his head.

"One night more, as I vowed," he grumbled to Kellory almost menacingly. "And no more! My warriors grow restive and unruly as ponies before a thunderstorm…hold them here, and they will slit our throats and carry off the girl to Novodny."

"I know," said Kellory. "One more night is all I need."

"To do what?"

"To trace the Evil to its lair, and destroy it," promised the dark man. The comical-looking little man studied him uncertainly.

"What help or weapons will you need?"

"Wax," said Kellory, taking a piece from one of the perfumed candles that lit Khun's field tent.

"Wax?" demanded the other incredulously.

Kellory nodded. Khun scratched his nose, baffled.

"Never will I comprehend the ways of wizards!" he said helplessly. Kellory smiled coldly, and stalked away.

* * * *

Kylix died in a welter of crimson upon the horizon. Shadows curdled into pools of purple gloom. Bonfires roared, roasting meat. Tribesmen feasted and drank, but with less appetite than usual. Kellory bade Carthalla seek her bedroll early.

"And take this," he said, handing her half the wax he had taken from the candle. She regarded him wide-eyed. He made a gesture with both hands toward his ears, and went swiftly away.

The chieftains posted their sentries, and none saw Kellory with his dark face and garments of black leather and long black cloak as he entered the shadows between the empty buildings. There he positioned himself where he could see but not himself be seen, and watched with the calm patience of a hunting cat.

The night sky deepened from vermilion to purple to the black of velvet. Stars blossomed forth like strewn handfuls of diamond-dust. One by one the three moons of Zephrondus floated up over the edges of the world. Silence lay thick as dust in ancient tombs upon the sleeping men, huddled beneath their quilted coverings; only the fires, as they crackled and spat, and the chill, uneasy wind, as it moaned through the broken walls, intruded upon the domain of stillness.

One of the sentries jerked around, facing darkness. His mouth fell open and he leaned forward, propped on his spear, as if listening intently. Kellory snapped to full alertness: the faintest whisper of sound came to him, like the murmuring of a distant voice. He dug two balls of candle wax from his purse, wadded them into his ears. The sound that had come to him had been thin and cold, like the icy winds of the Pole singing through spires of frozen crystal: but there had been an uncanny semblance of *words* in that whispery song, and in that moment it had seemed to the Warlock that he could almost make out the sense of them, if but he hearkened more keenly…now, his hearing blunted by the wads of wax, he could hear nothing of the insidious whispering.

But the sentry obviously could! The man was staring, Kellory noted, in a definite direction: the Warlock gazed beyond him, but he saw naught more than the well of gloom which lay in the narrow alleyway between two ruined structures.

Or—*was* there something amidst those shadows? He stared more intently, for now it seemed to him that the center of the darkness *curdled*, taking on substance…or was it only a trick of the triple moonlight and his tired eyes?

He glided from his place of hiding, a shadow among shadows, his steps soft and stealthy. For this once, the Warlock had exchanged his leathern boots for soft, supple buskins.

He could see the whites of the sentry's eyes, literally bulging from their sockets, staring with hideous intentness upon nothing, straining his ears to catch the rustle of mumbled words that just eluded his understanding. Working his way around a heap of rubble, Kellory momentarily lost view of the fascinated sentry. When he saw him again, the desert man had gone down on all fours, like an animal, like a mongrel cur. And, like a mongrel, he seemed to be whining or whimpering—the wax stuffed in Kellory's ears blunted the sounds he made to muffled gasps.

Curling in a tight ball, like a hound chewing on his hindquarters, suddenly—horribly—the sentry began eating of his own flesh.

Kellory's eyes blazed, green witchfire in the blackness. He sprang from the shadow of the wall, facing the curdled darkness squarely, and smote his Staff upon the broken pave. Its iron cap flared suddenly alight with electric blue-white glare, brilliant enough to scorch the eyes.

The thing within the darkness withdrew, retreated, dwindling down the black throat of the narrow alley. Holding aloft his Staff of Power, Kellory pursued, striding rapidly. Soon he, too, had vanished into the blackness. The odd thing about it was that none of the other sentries had noticed this swift turn of events; it was as if their senses were benumbed, as by some narcotic, while the Evil of this place struck down their comrade.

One alone, however, had watched the scene. It was the Sarkovy girl, Carthalla. She had but feigned slumber, watching for Kellory through slitted eyes. As she saw him spring from concealment and confront the thing that had goaded to madness the sentry, then vanish in the night, stalking his uncanny prey like a hunting cat, the Princess of Grand Khev came to her feet and hurried after the Warlock.

Going to what nightmare confrontation of magic pitted against magic she could not dream...

# CHAPTER 10

## THE SHADOWY THING

In the same instant that the Warlock brandished his Staff before the clot of darkness, and drove it fleeing from the actinic glare of his witch-fire, the spell that had held the Hawks of Khun bedazed ceased on a sudden. Khun himself shook his head and rubbed his eyes: had even he dozed off, when he should have been alert? Shamad threw himself at the old man's feet.

"Lord, the Whispering Death has driven mad the sentry, Uruzahn! Lord, we have put him out of his torment!" panted the chieftain.

Irritably, Khun nudged him with one booted toe. It was not a gentle nudge. "What of the Warlock, fool? Speak!"

"The Northman pursues the Death, and the woman pursues the Northman," stammered Shamad. Khun's eyes flashed.

"Aha! By the beard of my father, events begin to move! At last!" With a curt command to hold the men here, the old chief sprang upon his pony with an agility that belied his years. Seizing the reins, he tugged its head about in the direction to which Shamad pointed a trembling arm, and whirled off in a clatter of hooves.

The light of the three moons painted the undulant sands with dust-of-silver. Kellory followed the retreating thing out of the city, through a gap in the crumbling walls, and into the Sea of Sand. Ever it fled before the blaze of his Staff, and ever he pursued. His face was grim and merciless, his eyes like green-litten ice, lips clamped tight; it was even as he had guessed—the source of the Evil lay beyond the city, amidst the shifting sands. *That* was why the tribesmen had found nothing of importance within the walls…

From time to time, he caught a clear look at the thing. It had no real form or shape or substance; like a blotch of darkness, a smear of gloom, it was, a clotting of shadows, opaque near the center, but the edges were filmy, drifting and eddying like ink in clear water. But it was deadly, and dangerous beyond belief: an icy breath blew from it, frigid as the black wind that blows between the worlds, and the nearer he came to it, as it glided ever before him, his flesh crawled as to the foul contagion of some cosmic uncleanliness.

He knew it for what it was, now. The vital residue of some powerful intellect, gone mad with hate, strong beyond belief—strong enough to taint and stain the very earth of its resting-place with undying and cunning and sentient Evil.

And he knew its identity, although he could hardly believe it.

He followed it down the slope of dunes, and up the rise to the crest of the next. And cold fear touched his heart.

*O Azzamungandyr, Lord of the Mysteries*, he prayed to his god in the depths of his heart, *a fearful contest lies before me. And I have not recovered the fullness of my Power...!*

Then, and quite suddenly, the shadowy thing turned at bay, snarling soundlessly at him. It would go no farther...and even as he knew this, the blaze of unearthly radiance faltered and died, for truly Kellory had not regained his strength, and to maintain the flare further would have taxed his strength. He braced himself for the onslaught, but with little hope in his heart.

* * * *

Carthalla had doggedly followed Kellory from the city, although her throat was dry with terror and her heart hammered against the cage of her ribs like a wild bird. She could not have told you why she had done this rash thing, to follow the Warlock to the scene of his battle, for what was he to her, but an annoyance and a mystery?

But, since first the Thungoda slavers had intercepted the princess on her way to wed her royal betrothed, it was the grim dark man who had shielded her from hurt and harm. In this strange wilderness of men, magicians and monsters, Kellory was her only friend and ally. She could not have remained behind amidst the tribesmen, while he went forth alone to fight their common foe...

Reaching the crest of the dune, she paused, for there stood the Northman, brandishing his Staff as if it were a naked blade. And there, swooping down upon him like a mass of darkness, was the fearsome thing he had pursued. Even as she watched breathless, it surged upon him and enveloped the Warlock in its shadowy embrace. And at this, Carthalla started, lost her balance and fell rolling down the slope of the dune, to end shaken but unhurt at its base.

She had lost nothing but the lumps of wax she had stuffed in her ears. Searching about her in the moonwashed sand, she could not find them... but surely they were of no importance...

\* \* \* \*

As the shape of darkness flowed about him, Kellory strove to reignite his Staff; it but flickered feebly, sputtered, casting long, snapping sparks, then died. Truly, very much of his Power was drained.

It poured about him like some phantasmal fluid, and the touch of it was clammy, cold and wet, and noisome and unclean. It floated up to enhood his face, and the light of moons and stars was quenched, leaving Kellory alone and lost in the heart of utter and abysmal darkness.

The bitter cold seeped into his marrow, numbing his limbs and dazing his mind; his thoughts moved as sluggishly as did the blood in his veins.

And the whispering began.

# CHAPTER 11

## SORCERY AGAINST SORCERY

He could hear it, but faintly, like the echo of an echo; even thus, it gnawed at the edges of his mind, at the foundations of his sanity, and reason swayed, trembling. The unearthly cold drenched him through and through; the unendurable blackness blotted out even the memory of light. A loneliness so poignant as to resemble pain rose within him; a lost, abandoned hopelessness so virulent as to be like some disease of the soul threatened to drown and drag him down into the swirling vortex of nighted gloom.

Spell after spell he hurled at that which encompassed him, but to no avail. Cantrip after cantrip he uttered in a hoarse, croaking voice, through frozen lips. But the swirling tides of darkness sucked him down, and ever that accursed and damnable *whispering* nibbled at his sanity...

Then, of a sudden, the darkness ebbed about him. Moonslight gilt the sands. He sucked the dry, spiced air of the desert into starved, gasping lungs. His mind seemed frozen as his flesh, it slowly thawed and he looked blearily about him for the cause of his release.

Eyes blank and witless, Carthalla stumbled across the sands into the embrace of the waiting shadow.

Kellory could hear, however faint and far, the dim mutter of the whispering. And knew the girl was caught!

He was prone on the sand, although he never remembered having fallen. Now he lurched staggering to his feet somehow, swayed on numb legs, clawing for a spell that might banish the eager, trembling clot of blackness.

But found within him—*nothing*.

"Carthalla!" he yelled, his voice raw and painful. Oblivious to his presence, she stumbled forward, eyes fixed unwaveringly upon the hungry mass of darkness. And Kellory knew that the shadowy thing had withdrawn from him to assault the vulnerable girl, whose mind had no defenses against the damnable whisperings.

Within moments of time she would be a drooling, idiot thing. That fine, bright spirit—quenched! That clear, healthy mind—broken! That splendid young body—befouled!

Kellory drew himself up to his full height, lips compressed, eyes a twin blaze of green fury. From deeper within himself than ever he had reached till now, he tapped a source of strength even he had never known that he possessed. And the centers of his Power unleashed their thunders:

*"PNOMPHET!"* he roared, and the world shook beneath him. The darkness that lurked, trembling with eagerness, to enfold the staggering girl hesitated—recoiled—shifted its attention to the man-thing it had thought drained, numb, half-dead.

Kellory flung out his hand. Luminosity flared about his fingertips—strengthened—drew into focus!

From him gushed a flare of lightnings, brighter than a hundred suns. The desert lit to an unearthly dawn.

Carthalla cried out, shielding her eyes with shaking hands, fell to her knees.

Straight, and deep, into the very heart of darkness flashed that unendurable, that intolerable, spear of supernal fire.

And the darkness...*died.*

As a fragile blossom withers to the bite of frost...as the dew vanishes in the blast of noon...as the dawn of day dispels the dreads of darkness...the shadow shrank, grew lucent, vague, dim—and was gone!

Supporting his dead weight on his Staff, Kellory felt the strength drain out of him. His senses swam, his limbs trembled. He fought to hold tight to consciousness. Then, in a rush of thudding hooves, old Khun was there, hurtling from his saddle to support the Warlock, ease him to the earth.

"The girl," he mumbled between numb lips.

"She sleeps," grunted the desert chief, lifting a bottle to the Warlock's lips. "Drink, man!" Kellory drank, then fumbled at his garments. The old man felt, and found the slim silver case. He watched disapprovingly as the shaking hands guided crystalline powder to pinched nostrils. After a time, Kellory's feeble, faltering heartbeat steadied, grew stronger. His breathing became less labored and ragged.

Khun helped him to his feet. Leaning upon his Staff, the Warlock searched the dry sand.

"There!" he said, pointing. It was upon that spot that the shape of darkness had turned at bay, as if it could retreat no further.

Scraping aside the shallow sand, they found a stony tablet anciently traced with worn glyphs.

Kellory read the inscription aloud: *Thus doth Pnomphet the disciple of Yaohim mete out justice at last to the men Ashangabar that drave him forth to perish in the dry sands. Now have they fallen, even to the last babe, and of a swifter and more merciful death than was that to which they doomed him.*

Beneath the stone they found only withered bones and a clutter of ornaments and talismans. These were, however, of precious gems and noble metals, and assuaged the greed of Khun, who required some manner of treasure in order to justify this expedition. He was jubilant, capering and clowning, his fists full of glittering jewels; Kellory was somber. The Book of Shadows was not there.

But the Evil was laid to rest, forever.

* * * *

They returned to the city, Carthalla mounted behind Kellory, who swayed exhaustedly in the saddle, while Khun plodded on before, leading his shaggy pony by the reins.

Already they could see the effects of the destruction of the Evil. A red viper, thick as a man's forearm, glided across the rubble, coiling into shadows. As dawn broke, fire-golden, through the ruins, a lizard scuttled along the top of a wall. Almost, Carthalla fancied she could see mold and lichen growing in the dry cisterns.

The dead city was dead no more: Death had been dethroned here, and the life of the desert—gaunt, starved and meager though it was— flourished!

They rode back to the encampment of the tribe. The dark man swayed, half-dead with fatigue, in his saddle, but voiced no plaint. Khun was alive with excitement.

"You must rest, regain your strength," he chortled. "Then we will be as brothers—I will give you warriors to lead, and women to tend your tent." Kellory said nothing.

Khun laughed, and shook a bony fist at the morning sky.

"Let the princes of the world look to their thrones," he cried, "when the Wolf of the Steppes and the Hawk of the Desert ride—*together!"*

Kellory smiled.

# PART 4

## SHADOWS IN THE DARK

# CHAPTER 1

## GARDEN IN THE SAND

All day the great desert had baked in the heat of the sun-star, Kylix; now, towards the hour of sundown, purple shadows lengthened from the dunes and coolness entered the air.

Empty and dead lay the Sea of Sand, save for the small lives it nourished at its meager bosom. Scarlet lizards scuttled; desert-vipers lay somnolent in their cool, hidden lairs; a few carrion-hawks floated aloft against the fathomless blue.

A dark line of moving objects appeared on the horizon to break the monotony of this silent, grim and barren realm. As they came nearer, it could be seen that they were desert men in loose, flapping robes of black or dun or scarlet, called *allots.* Steel blades hung sheathed at waist and thigh, long spears were slung across broad shoulders, the gem-studded hilts of dirks twinkled from sash or girdle.

The shaggy ponies upon which the desert men were mounted had ridden long and hard: they stumbled, plodding through loose drifts of cinnabar-colored sand. And weariness lay in the dark, lean faces of their riders.

At the fore of this company there rode a remarkable personage. Thin as a starveling beggar was he, and remarkably ugly, although the eyes that peered from under tufted brows were wise and sweet and warm with humor. He possessed a huge, hooked nose and an extraordinary pair of mustachios, curled and waxed, from whose tips hung small, chiming bells of silver. His garments were complex, gaudy, almost comical in their excess of ornamentation. This was Khun, leader of the band of desert-raiders who had befriended Kellory the Warlock and the girl, Carthalla, and who were now escorting them through the Sea of Sand to a distant pass which led through the White Mountains into the lush meadowlands of Sarkovy.

Khun rode easily in his high saddle, chatting amiably, in high good humor. For all his years (visible in the iron-gray of his elaborately curled mustaches), the two days and nights of their journey through this harsh wilderness seemed to have left him untouched. Fresh and gay and relaxed was he, as if this were a mere outing.

But the blond Sarkovy girl swayed with weariness in the saddle, her lovely features pink with dust, blue eyes dull, lips dry and cracked. She ached in every muscle, and had become increasingly aware of muscles she had not known her slender body to possess.

As for Kellory, the grim silent man at her side showed no sign of tiredness; his hard, leathery features were immobile and unwincing, his witch-green eyes, narrowed against the burning shafts of sunlight, undulled. Alert and wary were they, and the grip of his one good hand on the reins was firm.

Khun observed the conditions of the two who rode at either hand with shrewd glances. He knew them for Northling-folk, unused to hard riding and the heat of the desert. Even as he glanced, the girl swayed over the saddle-bow, head down, wilted golden locks dangling from under the hood-like cowl of her desert robe.

"Soon we shall rest and be at ease," the old man crooned, giving her a merry smile. "And we shall drink deep and bathe in cool, fresh water!"

The girl searched the horizon with weary gaze. "Where, in all this burning waste, can such comforts be found?" she asked hoarsely.

Khun chuckled, eyes dancing. "Hard indeed is the Sea of Sand and hostile in many ways, but it has its hospitable side, too, as you shall see… for we will rest this night at a garden more beautiful than the Princes of Sarkovy may boast!"

Kellory and Carthalla looked inquiringly at him, but the old Hawk of the Desert said no more, chuckling with merriment at his small secret.

# CHAPTER 2

## A CRY IN THE NIGHT

They came to the oasis an hour before sunfall, and the sight of it was very welcome to Carthalla. As Khun had jestingly promised, the very sight of it was beautiful to the exhausted girl. Like a magical vision summoned by a conjurer, it seemed to melt into being before them, out of the sandy wasteland: a stand of feathery, blossoming trees encircling a pool like a mirror of sapphire.

Banks of dewy emerald moss sloped down to the margin of the pool, where tall reeds whispered, swaying to the touch of the evening breeze. The oasis was sheltered against the flanks of a tall, towering mass of stone, flat-crested like a mesa, but less large. In its shade, the garden flourished, drawing nourishment from hidden springs which fed the pool.

The desert-raiders dismounted gladly, leading their ponies to the mossy brink and letting them sink their muzzles in the cold, fresh water. Then, one by one, the warriors flung themselves on their bellies, lapping up the water like thirsty dogs. The Warlock and the Sarkovy girl drank more decorously, from cupped palms, but no less thirstily.

The sun-star died in a welter of crimson athwart the west, where dim mountains lifted against the first wan stars. Digging a pit, the desert men built a fire, roasting the fowl their bows had brought down during the day's riding. In the twilight they feasted on roast fowl, black bread, ripe olives, white cheese, red wine.

Saddlebags were unpacked; wains were unladen; tents of red-dyed felt were erected against the night-cold. Yawning hugely, Khun bade his chieftain, Shamad, assign the sentries. Kellory glanced at him with faint curiosity.

"What need for sentries, in this empty and accursed land?" he inquired. "Are there other tribes about, or savage beasts? If so, I have discerned no sign of either in all our journey hither."

Khun shook his head, small bells chiming sweetly.

"We have driven into the south, long ago, such tribes as shared the Sea of Sand with us," he crooned reassuringly. "And of beasts there are but few, and they no cause of fear to armed men in company. But the night holds other perils, and less wholesome…"

And, despite Kellory's repeated queries, the old desert chief refused to elaborate further on this odd remark.

\* \* \* \*

Kellory was roused suddenly from his slumbers and rose, staring about, his one good hand going out to touch the smooth and polished length of his long Staff, as a startled warrior reaches for his weapon. The echoes of the cry which had awakened him were still ringing in his ears. From her pallet, the girl looked at him, wide-eyed with alarm.

"Stay here, I will see what it is," he said shortly, rising to his feet. Not bothering to draw on his breeches and tunic of worn black leather, he went out naked into the night, to find others awake and up. The night-wind was cold on his lean body. He looked about, seeing naught amiss.

The startled cry had come from the youngest of the desert-raiders, a youth named Ahd. He had been posted at the very edge of the oasis, and now stood trembling, staring out over the dim stretch of the sands.

"What is it?" snarled Shamad, who had burst from his tent with bare steel in his hands. The boy stared at him, then with slow reluctance shook his head.

"…Shadows," he said from dry lips. "Shadows on the sand!"

"What *kind* of shadows, young oaf?" growled the chieftain impatiently. The boy shrugged, gesturing vaguely.

"…Huge…black…winged like great bats," he murmured.

Kellory looked up. The sky was clear and filled with blazing stars. None of the three moons of Zephrondus were yet arisen over the edges of the world, and the night was very dark.

"What is it that can cast shadows in the dark?" the Warlock inquired of Shamad. The other looked at him with a short, angry laugh.

"The shadows cast by too much wine, curse the youngling!" he snapped; then, with sharp words of reproof for the sentry, he strode back to his tent and vanished within. Kellory looked the youth over. The boy was obviously frightened by whatever it was that he had seen, but he seemed clear-eyed and steady on his feet, and they had none of them imbibed too freely of wine with their evening's feast.

"You saw nothing except shadows?" he asked. "Nothing in the sky to cast them? Heard nothing—felt nothing?"

The boy shook his head. In low, faltering terms he repeated what he had said to Shamad. He had seen huge, black, batwinged shadows drifting silently over the sands. *Shadows in the dark—?* Kellory frowned thoughtfully: shadows cast by—what? And by what uncanny light, as the night was dark and the desert steeped in gloom…

Shaking his head irritably, he returned to the tent he shared with Carthalla.

With dawn, it was discovered that one of the sentries was missing.

# CHAPTER 3

## WARLOCK ON WATCH

The missing sentry was a man called Yartha—unlike Ahd, a grown man, a seasoned warrior and a veteran huntsman, alert, wary and sober. Not a man to stray off into the night, or to start at strange shadows. He had vanished as if he had melted into empty air itself.

*"Ai,* Wolf!" grumbled old Khun, gnawing worriedly on his underlip. "It begins again, the sentries vanishing or going mad, as back in dire Ashangabar…you bring us ill-luck, Warlock!"

Kellory met his questioning eyes with a grim, somber glare.

"In Ashangabar, the peril was none of my doing, and I tracked it to its lair and slew it forever," he reminded the desert chief. "Even as I slew the mandragon who killed one of your warriors ere ever we reached the Dead City. Blame not these things on me, old Hawk—this desert is your land, not mine; and these dangers are yours."

Khun mumbled something under his breath, then nodded slowly.

"Aye, Black Wolf, your words are true, and old Khun spoke hastily, out of a troubled heart! In sooth, it is well we have a warlock with us, for this thing smacks of wizardry to me…and my men will face and fight fiercely against man or beast, but sorcery is not easily slain with steel. It takes magic to fight against magic."

Carthalla looked about her nervously. With a little shiver, she said, "We had no such troubles before, when we camped of nights amidst the sands…it is only this oasis that seems haunted by some nameless evil. Why, then, do we not mount up and begone, for it is day and night is a long time off?"

The old chief shook his head gloomily. "Tis not that easy a thing to do, my girl," he explained gruffly. "The desert is a merciless waste, where men and beasts will soon perish from heat and thirst, unless they are wise. We do not simply ride on and on, resting at night in our tents amidst the dunes: we ride from oasis to oasis, for we must consume more water than we can bear with us, we and our ponies. And they are nigh foundered. We must rest here for three days and nights, before venturing on, for there is only one more oasis between us and our goal in the mountains."

"For three more nights, then, we must face invisible things that carry men off in the dark of night, is that it?" the girl cried incredulously.

The ugly face of Khun was bleak, his thin lips tight-pursed.

"It is even so, I fear," he chirped. "Better a man or two should die, than the lot of us perish of wandering in the waste!"

The girl flushed crimson and turned abruptly away, tears in her eyes.

Kellory said nothing, his face drawn and hard.

That night he shared the watch.

\* \* \* \*

The sentinels this night were named Amoor, Rukh and Utha. Shamad himself, Khun's chief lieutenant, took the captaincy of the watch, which left Kellory free to roam from place to place on his own, without having to remain in one particular spot.

The sun-star died in crimson mists; the sky purpled to velvety blackness. Wan stars trembled, then brightened above the whispering sands. Nothing lived or moved out in the waste that Kellory's keen senses could detect; nothing hovered aloft against the stars.

Clad in black leather, wrapped in his great cloak against the nightchills, he lurked mostly within the thick heart of the tall feather-trees. Although he prowled from place to place about the perimeter of the oasis, he spent most of his time near the position at which Ahd had been stationed the night before. And most of his attention was fixed upon the undulant dimness of the desert, where the youth had seen, or thought that he had seen, the weird, drifting shadows.

An hour passed without occurrence. Then another went slowly by. Kellory set his back against the knobby trunk of a tall tree, leaned upon his iron-shod Staff and waited with grim patience for something untoward and strange.

The sentry posted near was the warrior named Rukh, a tall, long-legged man with a fringe of curling beard and eyes as sharp as any hawk's. The Warlock had seen this man face the terrors of the Dead City, and knew him for a stout-hearted warrior of iron will and stubborn courage. *It was, therefore, a surprise to him to hear such a man scream like a terrified woman…*

In an instant Kellory was at the side of Rukh, strong fingers seizing him by the shoulder. Rukh turned a face wet with cold perspiration towards the Warlock, dark eyes wide with amazed fear; with one shaking hand he pointed out into the gloom of the desert.

"…Shadows!" he whispered hoarsely. "Shadows in the dark—"

# CHAPTER 4

## INVISIBLE DEATH

Over the undulant surface of the gloomy desert there came gliding weird shadows, like moving pools of black ink. Kellory raised his head to rake the starry heavens with a swift glance: the skies were cloudless and clear. Nothing that could be seen with the eyes of the flesh there was that could have cast such shadows, and no source of illumination powerful enough to have made them upon the sands.

It was difficult to perceive the true shape and likeness of the things from the flat, two-dimensional shadows they cast over uneven surfaces of sand, but it seemed to him that they were like enormous bats, with low-browed, horned heads.

The eyes of the flesh...?

Growling a curse at his own stupidity, Kellory clamped his eyes shut, reaching within himself to the sources of Power. Behind the brows, between and just above the eyes, there is an organ vestigial in most men, but enlargened and no longer dormant in wizards, due to the disciplines of their craft. This Third Eye, the organ of astral vision, which perceives in a mode other than sight and requires no light-source on the physical plane for its visual perceptions, he opened—

*And uttered a startled cry.*

Without hesitation, he left the side of Rukh and advanced out onto the sands, black cloak flaring, witch-tangle of locks stirring on the breeze, magic Staff lifted as if to ward off some unseen evil.

And in the next moment, he had vanished as if he had never been!

\* \* \* \*

Others had been roused to action by the cries of Rukh, and the first among these to reach the scene were Shamad and Carthalla and old Khun. Shamad seized the frightened sentry by the arm and roughly demanded of him what had chanced to occur. In faltering tones, Rukh told them. When he was done, they stared at each other with wide, unbelieving eyes.

"Vanished into nothingness…can such things be?" murmured Shamad.

"As if swallowed up in the jaws of an invisible monster," whispered Rukh. "See, there," he added, pointing, "his footprints!"

They looked, and saw that the marks of Kellory's boots extended but a little ways into the sands before stopping short. They went nowhere: they simply…*ended.*

Khun shuddered, rolling his eyes superstitiously. In his time, the old Hawk of the Desert had seen many men die, and in many ways. But this eerie and invisible death that had claimed the Warlock was new and very terrible to him.

"We can pause here no longer," he muttered to Shamad in thin tones. "Bid the men mount up and let us begone from this accursed place!"

"But, Lord, see—the Shadows still rove!" gasped Shamad, pointing. The chief narrowed his eyes, then uttered a strangled cry. For it was so… well beyond the green edge of the oasis, the bat-winged shapes of darkness glided restlessly to and fro over the sands, as if lurking in wait for other unwary victims to venture out into their dim domain…

"Curse my shanks, I'm growing old," groaned Khun brokenly. "We must stay here until daybreak, at very least: but with dawn we ride!" This said, he stumbled back into his tent, before whose door stood the Nine Skull Standard of his ancient tribe.

Rukh stared into the desert at the drifting Shadows. "They circle like sharks about a boat, waiting for a fisherman to fall overboard," he said from dry lips. Carthalla shuddered, for it was even so.

"We dare not venture out into the desert to search for his remains," muttered Shamad, "not while those devil-things are there…"

Carthalla turned on Rukh. "Tell us everything that you saw," she demanded fiercely. "Any slightest clue may help! He may not yet be dead—and we cannot just abandon him to so dark a fate!"

Fumbling for words, the desert warrior again described the moment of Kellory's vanishment. And this time there occurred to him a detail he had left unmentioned, as it had seemed meaningless.

"You saw the Warlock's shadow joined with the devil-thing's?" repeated Shamad musingly. The sentry nodded vigorously.

"Then it seemed to dwindle, the double shadow of the two…as a hawk's shadow dwindles as it rises up into the air, after making its strike," said Rukh.

The chieftain rubbed his jaw thoughtfully.

"Hawks bear their kill back to their eyrie to devour at leisure," he said slowly. "But there are no hawks here, and no eyries…"

"There is the height," said Carthalla flatly. They turned to peer up at it, the tall chimney-like shape of rock, in whose shoulder the green oasis nestled.

"The crest seems too small to afford an eyrie to anything so huge as to cast so great a shadow," said Shamad dubiously. But the girl was as stubborn as she was defiant.

"Creatures with wings fly in the air, and roost in high places," she declared. "The mesa is the only high place hereabouts."

"Shall I rouse the warriors, my chieftain?" inquired Rukh. His fears were gone by now, and he hungered to prove his courage, if only to himself.

"For a fool's errand such as this?" grunted Shamad. "Never! We shall climb the steep ourselves, if only to prove the top empty."

"And I am going with you," declared Carthalla.

"You—a mere wench?" scoffed Rukh restlessly, eager for the adventure. "What can *you* do against the Shadows?"

"Little enough," admitted Carthalla. "But I can bear this to him, if he yet lives." And she pointed to the Warlock's Staff, a thin dark line against the sand, where it had fallen from its master's grip when he had been taken.

# CHAPTER 5

## THE HOLE

They climbed. The height was sheer and barren: neither moss nor mold nor lichen grew in the sharp gullies that furrowed the stone shaft from base to peak. It resembled nothing so much as the trunk of some colossal, cloud-touching tree, petrified over ages.

"If your band roams the waste, going from oasis to oasis," panted Carthalla as they paused briefly to catch their breaths, "why did you not know of the peril that lurks in this oasis?" Shamad shrugged.

"Not since our grandsires' time have we ventured this far into the west," he explained. "We know of the oasis only because it is marked on the most ancient charts. True, there was some writing near the mark on the map, but this we disregarded in coming hither..."

Carthalla suppressed a smile; she was well aware that the desert tribe could neither read nor write, but was too tactful to mention the fact.

They climbed farther.

When they reached the crest, they paused, amazed. For here, the top of the rise was not, as they had expected, a level mesa, but a mere lip. Before them, there extended into unknown depths the black throat of a crater-like well. The tower of stone was like a hollow chimney, save in that it was a natural formation, with nothing man-made about it.

They peered over the lip: exposed levels of stone strata could be seen, dwindling into the deeps, like a sort of ladder.

"There is life down there," whispered Carthalla. "See the light?" A sharp, metallic luminance glowed from below, an unnatural light, fierce as day but intense as some burning mineral.

"We can get down," murmured Rukh.

"Let us, then," said Shamad, and he slid over the brink and began to go down the steps which nature, it seemed, had cut into the many-layered rock. The others followed him.

As they descended the stone chimney, the weird blue light grew ever stronger. It seemed to radiate from slabs of strange minerals imbedded in the rock. These shed a strong luminance, like a natural phosphorescence.

They came to a ledge, where they rested. Beneath them, unguessable depths fell away, and an awful stench arose to assault their nostrils. The ledge was stained and streaked with oily droppings, as might be found beneath the roosts of unearthly birds. They descended farther.

Kellory they found huddled upon another ledge a bit farther down. The Warlock was unconscious, his leather tunic torn by claws, the flesh of his shoulder ribboned, a fearful gash on his scalp leaking rich blood on his face. For a moment they feared him slain; then the sensitive fingers of the girl, seeking beneath his torn leather tunic, found the beat of his heart, weak yet steady.

"He lives," she breathed. They reared him to a sitting position. After a moment or two, he blinked, looked around, became aware of them. In his cold green eyes was recognition, nothing more. Neither gratitude, nor relief, nor hope gleamed in those icy eyes.

"You were fools to come here," he whispered faintly, gesturing. They looked to see where spars of rock extruded from the throat of the chimney.

Upon these perched weird figures. They were bat-like, their great wings folded about them, adamantine claws clutching the rock on which they perched. But they were transparent, jelly-like, faintly visible even in the blue unearthly glare of the phosphoric minerals that alone gave luminance into this dark haunt.

The most horrible thing about them was that they had the faces of men and women upon their horrid bird-like bodies. Pinched and sharp and gaunt beyond the normal visages of humankind were these features atop the hideous, unhuman bodies of the bat-like things, but human they were, for all of that.

"They are dormant now," breathed Kellory in a faint voice. "The moons are up." Indeed, a many-hued luminosity flooded the cavernous space from the opening above: obviously, Sligon the Moon of Pallid Opal had risen.

"They are not made of matter as we understand the term," the War-lock murmured. "Light of any kind is, to them, a terrific and dangerous force. Only the mineral phosphorescence of this cavern are they able to endure. And only by its light are their bodies visible at all…"

"How do we get out of here?" grumbled Shamad, eyeing the dormant bat-creatures apprehensively. The moon would soon climb higher in the sky; no longer would its shifting, opaline luminance pour down the black throat of the shaft, to light this grim underworld and hold the bat-things at bay.

"Can you climb?"

Kellory struggled to a sitting position, but his strength was not sufficient to maintain it, and he sagged back, his face drawn. It was obvious that he was in great pain, and had lost much blood. He shook his head in silent reply to the chieftain's query.

"Here is Haklamaklan," said Carthalla, giving him the black Staff. "Can you not smite them with Power?" He smiled bitterly.

"I have already tried," he muttered. "I despise myself for this weakness, but the pain interferes with my concentration. I can try again, of course…"

Shamad and Rukh looked around restlessly. "If light hurts the things, mayhap we can make a fire," the chieftain said. Rukh scrabbled about in the gloomy corners of the cave, fastidiously avoiding the gnawed bones of men and beasts and the noisome, oily droppings. He found a plenteous supply of dry and withered leaves, blown by the winds from the oasis trees. He and Shamad searched their garments, but neither had brought flint-and-steel along.

"I have seen you but lay your hand upon wood and speak a Word to make fire," Carthalla said. "Can you not do so now?"

The Warlock tried, but no flame resulted from the attempt. It would seem that he must focus his mind upon such matters to effectuate them, and that the pain of his wounds broke every attempt at such concentration. Indeed, it was all he could do at times to maintain consciousness.

"What shall we do?" whispered the girl to the two desert men. Shamad licked his lips nervously.

"Whatever it is, we must do it quickly," he observed. "For they are awakening—"

# CHAPTER 6

## THAT WHICH DISPELS SHADOWS

Even as they turned, the opal radiance faded as the moon soared farther up the sky. And in the same moment, the hideous, jelly-like things stirred to wakefulness. Cold eyes blinked open, and it was horrible to see the bird-like rapacity that burned in those quasi-human faces.

Uttering shrill, raucous cries, the bat-things launched themselves from their perches, hurtling toward the man-creatures that had dared invade their nesting-place.

The men shouted and swung steel blades. These clove through the lucent bodies of the Shadow Bats without seeming to cause them hurt or harm. But, as the steel blades flashed in the waning moonlight, it could be seen that they flinched away from the flicker of luminance, veering off.

Then it was that Carthalla gasped as an idea struck her. She dug in the pocket-pouch at her side, and brought forth a small object which she held in the shimmer of the moonlight. It cast a narrow beam of fading light which caught the foremost of the Shadow Bats full in the breast.

It uttered an unearthly cry, almost too keen for the ears of men to hear, and before their astounded eyes the jellied flesh *crumbled*—rotting away as the light-beam bored into its weird substance. The jellied flesh bubbled and boiled, whiffing to a nauseous vapor. The crippled thing fell flopping, then moved no more. The rest of the flock fluttered into dark corners, cowering fearfully, squawking as if in horror.

Shamad blinked and swore, looking at the small thing Carthalla held cupped in her palm. He laughed shakily.

"Trust a woman to always have a mirror about her!" She grinned faintly, eyes alert for another launching-forth of the Shadows.

"Let us get out of here while we can," Rukh muttered. "I will rig a sling out of our cloaks, and we shall drag the Warlock up the shaft…and you, woman, be ready to drive them away again!"

\* \* \* \*

On the crest they paused to rest from their exertions, knowing that they had naught to fear from the horrors below so long as the Opal Moon was high. Indeed, Diostrion was rising, to add the strength of his emerald radiance to the light of the first moon.

The fresh night-air had partially revived Kellory from his swoon; now, as Carthalla staunched the dreadful wound on his brow and bound it with a strip of clean linen torn from the hem of her garment, he looked curiously at her, fully conscious.

"That was quick thinking," he said curtly, as near to a compliment as he had yet come. "To think first, and panic later—"

She smiled slightly, faint from the aftermath of fear.

"I am learning a few things from your example," the girl whispered.

They made it by slow stages down the slope to where Khun and his warriors awaited them. By the time they got to the bottom, the east paled and day was near.

"We seem always to be fighting—Shadows," said the girl, shivering slightly in the morning breeze. Kellory nodded, then winced as the motion tugged at the raw lips of his wound.

"These are creatures strayed or summoned hither from the Domain of Old Night and Chaos," he muttered broodingly. "In that dark realm, even shadows can slay. But fear not, for ever and aye, light will dispel the shadows."

Behind them the east flushed with gold as the dawn came forth to drive away the dark once again.

# PART 5

## THE SMILE ON THE FACE OF THE BEAST

# CHAPTER 1

## THE MOUNTAINS WHITE AS DEATH

Kellory and the girl, Carthalla, stood and watched as Khun, and the Riders of Khun, dwindled into the distance across the ochre desert known to men as the Sea of Sand. Then the two turned their faces northwards and began their slow ascent of the mountain pass which led across the White Mountains into the grassy plains of Sarkovy.

"They were good friends," the girl sighed, shivering a little at the caress of the cold winds that whistled down from the heights. The gaunt, grim man who strode at her side made no response. To his way of thought, every hand was lifted against his own, until the owner of that hand became a proven friend. And the desert-raiders were no different from the rest of the world; they had been tested, and the metal of their souls had been proven in the fires. But they had been comrades, rather than friends...

For too long had the Warlock, and the woman he had rescued from the Thungoda slavers, wandered in the depths of the vast deserts of the south. The treasure, whose search had brought them first into these parts, had again eluded them, while they strayed afar on strange paths. And now the trail seemed lost. There remained little else for them to do, but to return to Sarkovy in hopes of finding another clue to the whereabouts of the lost Book of Shadows.

They toiled up the steep, rocky road of the pass with Kellory lending a hand to help Carthalla over the rougher places. Although both were weary from days in the saddle, what time the Hawks of Khun had escorted them across the Sea of Sand to the foot of the Azun Pass, Kellory pressed on without pause to rest. The reason for this was that these mountains enjoyed a poor reputation among travelers, and the Warlock did not wish to discover the reason for the ill rumors that had come to his ears. He wished to reach the relative safety of the plains before the sun-star Kylix died in its bed of crimson coals against the west.

They climbed. Here winds blew fierce and chill off the bleak heights of harsh, chalk-white stone. White as death itself were these stark and stony peaks, which seemed in itself a strange, even an unnatural, thing.

But Kellory had heard of these White Mountains during his days of apprenticeship under the tutelage of Phazdaliom the Green Enchanter, and he knew that there was more that was unnatural about this range than merely its hue. Little there was that lived among these gaunt crags, and little of that which could be considered wholesome.

But they had come this far unscathed, and would venture even farther, trusting in their gods.

At the top of the pass they were forced to rest a few moments in order to catch their breath. They stared down at the green plains of Sarkovy; many small streams watered that verdant meadowland, serving as tributaries to the great river that arched off to the north, drowned from sight in the mists of distance. The white walls of the city Novodny, which was their goal, lay not far off beyond the foothills of the mountains, surrounded by farmhouses with smoking chimneys, and broad, well-irrigated fields. Here, in view of their goal, they rested, munching cold rations from the saddlebags Kellory carried, assuaging their thirst with draughts from a waxed wineskin filled with the strong brew of the desert-raiders.

As they rested, Carthalla cast surreptitious glances at the grim and silent man who companioned her; of him, and his ways, she knew so very little, for all the many days they had spent together, living cheek by jowl, as close as lovers, but never touching. He was a great mystery to her, this silent, brooding man with the one good hand, the other a crippled stump covered in its tight glove of black leather. But they had ventured far together, and had found a certain measure of comfort, if not of ease, in each other's presence.

Kellory was relieved to set down his burden, and he piled the bags beside the road to stretch leather-clad, strong shoulders and seize a moment's respite from the climb. The shaggy, behorned ponies they had taken from the Thungoda raiders were of no use to them on this steep road, hence these they had given over into the hands of Khun and his Desert Hawks.

From here on, they knew, perforce they must go afoot, bearing upon their own backs their burthens. Nor was the way lessened thereof, for the road was hard and they wearied easily at this height, where the air was bitter cold and very thin. And especially did the Warlock tire easily, for his strength was drained from his recent magical exertions in the Dead City of Ashangabar.

Carthalla looked wistfully at the red roofs and tall towers of the walled city which lay not far off amidst the grassy plains.

"Have you ever been to Novodny?" she inquired, having caught her breath. Kellory shook his head expressionlessly.

"Never; but soon we shall explore it," he said. She glanced curiously at him.

"What do you hope to find in Novodny?" she inquired. The dark man shrugged.

"Pnomphet left his disciples, who survived his demise," he said in somber tones. "We know they outlived him, for it was by living hands that the inscription was cut into the stone slab of his tomb. With the doom fallen upon Ashangabar, there would have been no place for them to seek refuge in, save for the cities of Sarkovy. And the first of these which we will search is Novodny, southernmost of the Seven Cities."

"But where will you look? Of whom will you ask—and what?"

He frowned irritably at all this talk, for he was a solemn and a silent man, who kept his own counsels and disliked idle chatter.

"I will ask of the wise men and the magicians," said he, "if they know aught of the followers of Pnomphet. If they do not, then we will look elsewhere…"

She parted her bright lips to ask further of him, but he rose suddenly and grasped her arm, motioning for silence. She stared around her at chalk-white walls and the dusty, rock-strewn path, seeing and hearing nothing.

And then it came again, that which had before been too faint for her to hear.

"What *is* it?" she whispered.

He said nothing, straining to hear. And then a third time there sounded an eerie, moaning cry, as of some hurt thing begging to die…

# CHAPTER 2

## SHADOWS THAT SLAY!

"It sounds like a child—a child in pain!" cried Carthalla breathlessly. And, shrugging off the restraining arm of Kellory, the girl strode across the rocky mouth of the pass, looking about, one small, capable hand clenching the hilt of her keen dagger. Kellory sighed, rose, shrugged and followed her, unlimbering his long black Staff of carven wood.

"There—" hissed Carthalla, pointing down the slope. He looked, to see something like a crouching shape, huddled under a shabby cloak.

Then he blinked, and looked again, seeing only a shadow where the form had been. Then even the shadow was gone. He turned to speak to the girl, but she brushed past him, clambering lithely down the slope.

"It *is* a child! A lost child, maybe hurt—come on!" cried Carthalla, scrambling down the rocks. Small stones, dislodged by her careless feet, went clattering and bouncing down the steep incline. Kellory groaned, growled a crude expletive under his breath and hastened after her. But when he came to where the shape had crouched, nothing at all was there.

"There it is!" cried Carthalla, pointing. He stared, to see the shabby shape huddled forlornly farther down the slope. It seemed to be shivering in fear, and there came to his hearing again that mournful, despairing cry.

"Carthalla!" he said, trying to halt her. But it was as if that pitiful, huddled bundle of rags had aroused within her breast every maternal instinct, for the girl was determinedly climbing down the rockface to where the shivering, small shape clung, whimpering. She ignored his cry as if she could not hear it.

As he came scrambling after her, his progress hampered by the saddlebags he carried slung across his shoulders, she descended to where the pitiful bundle of rags lay trembling and moaning. She uttered soothing words as she stooped to pluck at the dirty rags—Shadows soared!

The bundle of rags exploded into a towering, dim shape, all lean torso and long, lunging arms—but vague, lucent, gray, as transparent as a shadow. Carthalla screamed.

The shadow-thing swooped down to encircle her in its misty arms, voicing again that mewling cry, which now had coarsened into a snarl of menace. But even as it reached to embrace the shrinking girl, Kellory was there, his long Staff outthrust, its metal cap blazing suddenly into a dazzling flare, stronger than the sun.

"*Go back, Shadow*!" he commanded in a deep voice that rang like thunder among the hills. "By the Name ZUOLNUMATHON, I bid you withdraw from us—"

The shadow-shape shrank back, whimpering, drawing filmy webs of shadow-stuff across the place its eyes should have been, as if the searing actinic light caused it agony. But something—hunger, perhaps—made it linger, still lusting for the girl it had almost entrapped.

Kellory uttered another Name, and whirled the Staff about his head in a whistling circle. It drew a circle of blue-white fire upon the air—a circle which did not die, but hung crackling, spitting sparks. One tendril of the shadow-thing touched the fire-circle, and it recoiled with a screech.

Then suddenly another voice was added to his own, a deep, booming voice that repeated the incantations even as he uttered them. Under the doubled burden of this wizardry, the shadowy menace shrank, dwindled, and was gone as if it had never been.

Carthalla collapsed sobbing into Kellory's arms. Cold green eyes wary and vigilant, the Warlock looked beyond her to the tall, robed man who stood behind them on the flinty path, and whose strength had aided him in the contest.

He was old, his face seamed with furrows of thought and care, his bald pate crowned with gossamer wisps of snowy hair, his eyes deep, thoughtful, full of wisdom. About his thin neck, dangling upon his bony chest, a small figurine of blue paste caught the eye of Kellory, and the Warlock relaxed; almost, he smiled.

"I had not thought to find another of the Brotherhood of Darkness, here amidst these barren and accursed peaks," he remarked, making a certain Sign with the fingers of his one good hand.

"Well for you and the maid that you did," said the old man gruffly. "For among these peaks lurk shadows...shadows that slay."

Carthalla shivered, staring wide-eyed at the old man. "I—I thought I heard a lost child, hurt and frightened," she said, faltering. He nodded wisely.

"They mimic the cries of frightened children, to lure the unwary to a Doom whereof I will say no more, save that it is not a wholesome way to die." He straightened, peering around; darkness had fallen and the west swam in a sea of crimson fire. "Night is upon us, and shadows love the dark," said the old man. "Come, there is a warm fire in my hut upon the heights, and food and a place to spend the night."

"Can we trust him?" whispered Carthalla to Kellory. He bared white teeth in a wolfish grin.

"I would rather trust him than spend the night on these shadow-haunted peaks," he said.

# CHAPTER 3

## WORDS ON THE HEIGHTS

The name of the old man was Temgis, and he was, as Kellory had surmised, a member of that worldwide fraternity of wizards, the Brotherhood of Darkness. Although he had long ago retired from the world, seeking a lonely place to meditate and strengthen his spirit among the cold peaks, far from the temptations of the plain, he had not lost his Power through disuse, as he had proven there on the slope, when he had joined his will to Kellory's in putting down the shadow-shape.

The hut of Temgis was larger than it looked, and more comfortable than it might have been. The old wizard had built it of stout wooden beams, their chinks caulked with dried clay against the winds, and it set its back against the sheer side of a cliff, where it caught the morning light. Inside, a fire roared on a broad stone hearth, and the walls were hung with rich cloth in heavy folds, which also served to keep out the dank chill of the heights. From the rafters hung bundles of herbs, strings of red and green peppers, white onions, sides of salted meat. The floor was warmly and thickly carpeted.

"You do yourself comfortably, brother, for one who has retired from the world!" remarked Kellory. Carthalla looked at him, faintly surprised: it was the nearest thing to a jest that the grim man had ever spoken in her presence. Temgis smiled, pouring hot mulled spice-wine into wooden bowls.

"Old bones require a cozy nest," he chuckled. "Come, drink, eat, rest yourselves! For I perceive you have come from afar."

He looked squarely, frankly into Kellory's witch-green eyes, weird in his gaunt, bronzed face, framed in its tangle of black locks.

"I have heard much aforetime of the Warlock with the One Hand!" he murmured. "And naught that should make him unwelcome in my home."

Kellory nodded as if acknowledging the recognition. "And I have heard of one Temgis of the Nine Books, that was high in the Second Circle of the Brotherhood, before he retired from the lands of men, to ponder upon his soul like a hermit."

Temgis smiled deeply into Kellory's green gaze.

"We know each other, then," he said softly.

* * * *

That night, after supper, stretched out before the fire, they talked a little, while Carthalla drowsed. Kellory thought it over, then decided to tell the old wizard of his mission. The bald brows of Temgis frowned at the mention of the Book of Shadows.

"Somewhat I have heard of it, indeed, ere this," he growled. "But naught that is healthy to the body or soul of men; beware how you wield the power locked in those dark pages, lest you loose some thing that may turn and rend you."

"I will remember that," said Kellory, "when I have the Book in hand, for as yet I have not found it. In sooth, I do not even know whether it still exists or not."

Old Temgis shrugged, grimacing. "Better it had perished with great Yaohim," he muttered. "Or with Pnomphet, his disciple, as perhaps it did."

"Perhaps," said Kellory, smiling. "But if it survived the death of Yaohim, then mayhap it survived the death of Pnomphet, as well! Some books have longer lives than do the men that wrote them, I have heard."

Temgis rubbed his brows in thought. "Dzimdoul was the first of the students of Pnomphet," he mused. "It was before my time, of course; but something of his papers were preserved…"

"Where?" asked the Warlock bluntly.

"There is a great library in the city of Novodny," began Temgis, and Kellory smote his brow.

"The Archives of the Ages," he breathed, mouth twisting bitterly. "Of course! I knew some wisp of memory whispered that I should seek first in Novodny, but I could not think why, save that it was first to hand."

They talked on; eventually, they slept while great winds rose and howled about the heights.

# CHAPTER 4

## BANNER OF THE MANTICHORE

With dawn the two bade farewell to their host, and departed to seek the plains of Sarkovy. Carthalla was not sorry to leave these cold white peaks where shadows roved and ravened, but Kellory cast many a backwards glance at the stout-walled hut, wistfully dwelling upon its loneliness and its peace. Perchance, when all his toils were done, and if the Lords of Life spared him, he, too, could find a measure of peace in some secluded hermitage, such as that in which the wise Temgis would spend his declining years…

He frowned, shrugging off these comforting thoughts of a peaceful old age. There would be no peace for him till he had seized the Book of Shadows, unlocked the riddle of its pages, and used its mighty power to banish the bestial Thungoda from this fair, green land, in vengeance for his own slaughtered people.

Striding along beside him, Carthalla stole a shy glance at the bleak, half-averted face of her tall companion. She felt like chattering, for her heart was lighter as they left the stark white cliffs behind; but she shuddered at his look, and wisely held her tongue.

They descended to the lush plain. By midday they reached the gates of Novodny, and went in.

They found the city a bustling, busy place, crammed with soldiers. The narrow and cobbled ways were crowded with merchants, farmers and hawkers, for this was Market Day. Kellory clove a path through the jostling mob and found them lodgings at an inn near the Prince Arahkh Bazaar, although Carthalla protested at this needless expense, a drain on a purse already lean.

"As the daughter of the High Prince of Grand Khev," she argued, "I will be a welcome guest in the palace of the Prince of Novodny, and so will you, as my companion and guardian."

"Are you acquainted with the Prince of Novodny?" inquired the Warlock. Reluctantly she shook her head, bright hair tousling over bare shoulders.

"Then you are better off at the inn," he said bluntly. "Such as Prince Parlion are best avoided by young women." He strode off to settle with the innkeeper, leaving her staring puzzledly after him. What was there about Prince Parlion that she had to fear? She frowned, then shrugged: the ways of this grim, silent man were beyond her.

Carthalla noticed, but dismissed, a furtive, rat-faced little man in shabby black who was watching her closely from the farther end of the ale-room in which Kellory had left her. He was looking her up and down with sharp, narrowed eyes in a manner suggestive of a surreptitious leer.

Aware of the rents in her travel-worn garments, which permitted generous glimpses of bare flesh to be visible, the girl flushed and averted her eyes from the watchful little man. Soon she forgot his very existence, as attractive young women soon become accustomed to being looked at admiringly by men. She went up to their room to unpack, and thus did not see the little man as he slunk from the room when Kellory's back was turned.

Nor did she mention this occurrence to the Warlock—an omission for which she was later to pay dearly…

They washed, ate, rested. Then it was time for Kellory to be about his business.

"I shall be at the Archives, it may be, most of the day," he instructed her. "Wait for me in our rooms, and do not open the door to anyone but myself." Then he was gone.

At the corner he paused, while a troop of well-armed soldiery marched past under the standard of a golden beast unfamiliar to him. He watched a bold, laughing-eyed man in rich armor ride past on a finely caparisoned steed, nonchalantly accepting the huzzahs of the citizenry. "Who is that lord?" Kellory asked of a merchant in green silk standing near. The man stared at him, beady eyes curious in his doughy, plump face.

"Why, fellow, that is Duke Almery, the Guardian of the Realm, riding under the banner of the Golden Mantichore; surely a familiar face in these parts by now! He has drawn the legions in to arm for a campaign against the Thungoda hordesmen—"

Kellory's green eyes sparkled with alert interest. For it was certainly news to him that any of the lords or monarchs of the Seven Cities were as yet concerned about the bandy-legged little hordesmen filtering down from the North in ever-increasing numbers. He inquired further.

The merchant shrugged. "Sounds like nonsense to me! But the Duke argues that the Thungoda will overrun all of Sarkovy, unless halted now. Already they lie encamped on the plain south of Grand Khev."

"And what do they in the lands of the High Prince?"

"Oh, I've heard they negotiate with the Prince of Khev for land-rights for their herds, buying land with promise of much gold when their leader, Black Mnar, comes down from Barbaria."

With that, the merchant re-entered his stall, leaving Kellory alone with his thoughts.

# CHAPTER 5

## THE SMILE OF THE BEAST

The famous Archives were a block of tile-roofed buildings set amidst flowering gardens. Cool arcades of columns marched in a row, casting shade wherein lazed scholars and students from Gorovod and Skhvar, Arungol and Kavlad, Ordovoy and even Grand Khev itself, as well as from easterling Aijan and the trade-cities of the Hundred Isles, and some were even come hither from the Gold City, so far to the jungled south as to be deemed nigh fabulous.

This was only fitting, as within these tall buildings of white marble reposed the greatest collection of books and scrolls and incised tablets ever amassed in the history of man. It was Prince Udrun of the Borgovoy Dynasty had begun the mighty collection, added to by each successive Prince of Novodny after his time. It was a common saying in Sarkovy that if a book did not repose in the Archives at Novodny, it was not worth preserving at all.

"The Thaumaturgical Collection is in the Great South Rotunda," said a harried clerk in answer to Kellory's request. "That is just beyond the Quad, near the Geographical Librarium. You will know the Rotunda from the Malachite Obelisk that stands before it, a gift from the Matriarch of Kavlad." Kellory nodded and left.

Before the Rotunda, he found a small academy of students at the feet of the philosopher Therion, whose works he had himself studied. For the most part, these were languid, effete, perfumed young intellectuals of the aristocratic Khyon class; he lingered to overhear their conversation, for they were talking about the Thungoda menace, and, for the most part, were deriding Duke Almery as an hysteric.

"The Thungoda are peaceful, simple children of the northern steppes," one young exquisite was explaining. "They worship their sky-gods and hunt the great deer of the steppe. Military conquest is an art beyond the scope of their intellects, why, the tactics alone—"

"They wrought considerable conquests in Barbaria, in my youth," said Kellory, interrupting. The other cast him an amused glance, taking in his lean height and worn black leather.

"The Warlord, Mnar, is a man of peace; his emissaries explain that all he requires of Sarkovy is the rental or purchase of land for his herds. These they will buy with red gold—"

"They will buy the lands they want with swords," said Kellory bluntly, "red with the blood of the men and women of Sarkovy, if you be not wary!"

At this juncture, the philosopher spoke up. He knelt tailor-fashion on a red cushion a bit higher up the marble steps than his academy of students.

"I perceive, sir, that you hew to the line proposed by our gallant Duke of the Realm. And I dare conjecture that neither he, nor you, can explain why Mnar offers to buy lands, if he can seize them at sword-point?"

"Certainly," said the Warlock. "He buys time to allow more of his horde to descend from the North, to swell his ranks. Then, when all is ready, he will pick a quarrel with the Prince of Grand Khev on some pretext, overrun his kingdom, and put all to the sword—while explaining, through his emissaries, to the other Princes, that the argument is but between him and Khev, and poses no threat to the neighboring kingdoms."

The philosopher smiled incredulously, saying nothing; but the young nobles were less polite, and made jests to each other, in a voice just loud enough to be heard, mocking Kellory's northern accent. His face tight, the Warlock turned on his heel and strode within the Rotunda, cursing within the silence of his heart. "There are none so deaf as those who will not hear," was the proverb that echoed in his thoughts.

He looked around: shelves of beautifully written vellum books stretched from floor to ceiling in the cool, hushed shade of the domed Rotunda. Poets and scholars sat at long, polished tables, perusing the books and scrolls. Here and there on pedestals stood lovely sculptures of alabaster or marble or bronze, depicting the Spirits of Thought and Contemplation.

It galled his breast that this loveliness, this learning, which basked now in timeless serenity, should be trampled into running slime and blackened rubble, when the Thungoda came.

He turned to consult after the papers of Pnomphet, to discover they were not preserved in this collection; neither were the effects of Dzimdoul, his first disciple. At length, he found a memoir of Dzimdoul by one Urush, who had been a student of Dzimdoul. Studying it closely, he found a curious passage whose meaning seemed to relate to the matter in question, but did so in such veiled and ambiguous terms as to be incomprehensible. It read:

> ...And they carried hither with them into Sarkovy the Book of Yaohim the Wise, the which now lieth hidden behind the smile of the Ghaast.

Kellory stared at the page with frowning brow and glaring eye, as if to wrest from it by sheer concentration the secret that it hid from him. The passage told of the flight from Ashangabar by the followers of Pnomphet, led by the eldest of the disciples of that mage, Dzimdoul. They had come across the White Mountains by the Azun Pass, and up the River Road to Ombor, turning west to Novodny. All of this, or much of it, Kellory had already guessed. And that they had carried with them the Book of Shadows had been his hope, now confirmed: but where was it hid?

Now the Ghaast was a beast of myth, the guardian of the Mysteries and the emblem of secrecy, of all that is occult and hidden and, thus, unknown. The enigmatic and unreadable smile upon the face of the beast was symbolic of that which was arcane and concealed from the knowledge of men. Therefore, to say that the Book was hidden behind the smile of the Ghaast was to say that it was unknown...

He left the Archives with a feeling of deep hopelessness such as he had never heretofore known, even in his moments of deepest despair. For it seemed to the Warlock that his last hope was gone, and his mission an idle thing.

# CHAPTER 6

## THE EARS OF THE MANTICHORE

On impulse, Kellory did not at once return to the inn where the girl Carthalla awaited his coming, but turned into Great Square Street, and sought the Iophantine Palace, the residence of Duke Almery. This noble, of whose fame as a war-leader even Kellory had heard, was the only aristocrat of the Seven Cities who seemed aware of the menace of the Thungoda, and the Warlock desired to have speech with him.

He found the palace a busy place, with pages and messengers coming and going, and officers standing about in small groups, talking in low tones to each other. After cooling his heels for the better part of an hour, Kellory was at last admitted into the presence of the Duke, whom he found bent over a great desk on which lay outstretched a vast, minutely detailed map of the plains south of Grand Khev.

Almery was a huge blond bear of a man, with ice-gray eyes and a magnificent mane of golden hair. His complexion was ruddy, his features jovial, his voice a hearty, booming one. He turned a brief glance to Kellory, whose bow he acknowledged curtly with a slight nod.

"Sir, you have pleaded a moment's discourse with us in regard to the Thungoda; pray be brief, for many others wait," he said crisply. Kellory nodded; in short words, he explained himself and his mission. The Duke blinked, and stared at him.

"We have heard of this arch-wizard of yours, my man," he remarked. "And even of his Book, whose power is a thing of legend in these parts... but the scheme you describe amazes us...you will be the same dark man with green witch-gaze who harangued the academy of Therion this morning on the steps of the Great South Rotunda..."

Kellory's eyes sparkled with mischief. "The ears of the Mantichore are long, indeed," he murmured. The Duke grinned hugely and guffawed.

"Let us say, the Mantichore has many servants in many places," he said. "They keep their eyes open, as well as their ears."

The two men talked, the Duke keenly eager to learn all that Kellory could tell him of the Thungoda and their ways. At length, the Duke regretfully terminated the conference.

"Our Prince has yet again deferred the meeting we have sought," he said bitterly. "There remains no further purpose for us to remain here, languishing in antechambers, while the Thungoda gather on the plain in all their thousands. With the dinner hour we shall be on our way north with our troops; if you will ride hither with us, we shall enjoy the augmentation of our strength with your thaumaturgical skills. If not, then fare you well!"

"And fare you well, my Lord Duke," responded Kellory. "There seems naught left for me to do but join with you in the battle, and you will see me there. I shall join you on the road north, perhaps."

He left the Iophantine and hurried through the long shadows of afternoon to the inn. On his way through the ale-room, hunger overtook him, for he had not partaken of nourishment that day. He paused long enough to feast frugally on pepper soup, brown bread, and toasted sausages, washed down with a beaker of honey-ale. Then he went up to their rooms.

And found Carthalla gone.

* * * *

Kellory stormed downstairs to demand of the innkeeper what had befallen his companion. The shrewd-eyed proprietor fended off his questions easily.

"The Prince's Guard came, a sergeant and four troopers, to fetch her off for 'questioning'," the fellow explained.

"What is meant by 'questioning'?" demanded Kellory. The innkeeper grinned knowingly, and tipped Kellory a conspiratorial wink.

"Oh, *you* know—!" he chuckled, leering. "Our pretty Prince has a nice taste for young women of certain, ah, enticements…here, where are you off to?"

"To fetch my lady back," said Kellory harshly. The innkeeper gaped at him.

"Are you mad?" he whispered. "By this time our gentle Parlion has her at his summer villa by the river…you would be a fool, or worse, to interrupt him at his 'pleasure'—"

But, with a swirl of his black cloak, Kellory strode out the door and was gone.

# CHAPTER 7

## THE TOWER OF GLASS

Kellory packed, slung his saddlebags over the cruppers of a hastily purchased pony and rode out of the gates of Novodny into the North. His brain was a seething turmoil of thoughts. If he paused to attempt the rescue of Carthalla, he might miss Duke Almery, who would be riding further north to Grand Khev. And gone would be his best chance of leaguing with the one strong leader in all of Sarkovy who appreciated the peril of the Thungoda, and planned to do something about it.

On the other hand, he could not just abandon the Princess to the nameless fate that awaited her, for all men knew what became of one of Prince Parlion's playthings when he had tired of his toy…

"Curse the wench!" he snarled, tugging the pony about and clattering up the River Road towards the pleasure-villa of the Prince. There was nothing else to do but try to save Carthalla—although what one man could do against the Prince's Guard he did not know.

* * * *

It grew darker; the moons ascended the clear sky one by one, their colored light alleviating the purple shadows. Kellory rode north with the speed of an avenging demon, his wizard's cloak flying out to either side of his hurtling form like the black and flapping wings of an enormous bat, his green eyes burning through the murk like twin lanthorns.

He cantered past farmhouses with smoking chimneys, surrounded by plowed and irrigated fields; groves of standing trees and some of the small lakes that dotted this southern meadow-land like many round mirrors under the moons.

Soon the river curved into view, the broad and rushing Turisan, like a silver scimitar under the glittering stars. Here along the riparian esplanade rose the turreted mansions and villas of the nobility, a great standard flowing in the wind from the topmost tower of each edifice. Here lolled the wealthy merchants and aristocrats, enjoying the cool breezes from the distant sea during the hottest days of summer. And here they enjoyed the protection of their hired guards, as well.

To avoid the armed bands that watched the road and warded all approaches to the stately mansions, the Warlock took to the fields and rode overland, seeking the shelter of the forests that dotted the plain. None saw or heard him pass, the hooves of his horned pony muffled in the soft grasses, his dark shape of no more seeming substance than a flying shadow cast by a floating cloud...

He came at length to the outskirts of the Prince's villa.

It was a cluster of rambling structures, centered about a soaring spire of glittering metal, paned with huge curved windows of rare crystal. Transparent as glass seemed that faerie tower in the dimness of night.

Gorgeous gardens surrounded the tower of the Prince on three sides; on the fourth, sloping flights of broad steps descended by tiers to the river's shore, where a pleasure-barge floated at the mooring, its gondola-slender form festooned with ropes of woven blossoms.

Here there were many guards, and wary sentinels, and ponies tethered near roaring fires where the off-duty watchmen passed the hour.

Here he must go slowly and carefully, for it would never do to risk discovery now.

Dismounting, Kellory tethered his steed behind a stand of flowering trees, and, wrapped in his black cloak, whose color blended with the night, he crept forward on silent, furtive feet.

# CHAPTER 8

## A THIEF IN THE NIGHT

Kellory skulked about the perimeter of the circle of guards, but could discover no way past them. Bonfires blazed, cutting through the murk, and sentinels strode their rounds with alert and wary eyes, swords or pikes held at the ready. Even a slinking water-rat could hardly have penetrated their lines unglimpsed...

Kellory crouched behind a glossy-leafed bush, considering alternative plans of action. Then, as there seemed no other way to gain entry to the palace of glass, he drew from his pouch of periapts and amulets a small box of ebony, wrapped in a silken kerchief. Opening this with a whispered Word, he carefully drew forth a ring fashioned from fragile ivory, set with a large stone of elusive, shifting hues. This odd ring he placed upon his thumb.

It was called a Ring of Gyges, and was a rare talisman of High Magic he had purchased from a master-mage who dwelt in the Ghoul-Haunted Hills of the North, ere ever he had met the girl Carthalla.

Kellory focused his attention upon the ring, reaching down into the depths of his Power to tap the energies stored there. In the shifting colors of the moonlight, the strange runic signs cut into the surface of the opalescent gemstone gleamed as if graven with a pen of liquid fire: the symbols burned into his consciousness, touching to life chords of empathetic response.

Under his breath, the Warlock uttered a Name.

His form blurred, became lucent, then as transparent as a piece of glass.

For a moment, all that could clearly be seen was the outline of his body, cut against the darkness. All within that sharp silhouette was like a swirl of eddying smoke...then steam, a rippling of the air.

Then he was gone, as if he had never been.

\* \* \* \*

Invisible, Kellory glided through the underbrush towards the princely palace. Bushes swayed, leaves crackled, as his viewless form slid through them.

He went silent and unseen through the circle of the watch-stations and past the stalking sentries. There was no sign of his passage, save for those small signs too unobtrusive to be noticed even by the most vigilant: grass blades crushed flat to earth underfoot, the faint rustle of his cloak as the wind caught its folds.

Through the gardens he glided like a thief in the night, and circled the rambling out-buildings, approaching on swift and silent feet the inner citadel that soared against the stars like a minaret of glinting ice.

He neared the portico, where tall windows gave forth upon a view of sumptuous carpeting, piles of plump pillows, smoking braziers of blue incense, tiny tabourets of oily black wood, laden with copper bowls of ripe fruit, fresh-cut blossoms, sugary cakes, tall crystal decanters of golden wine.

A window edged ajar. An unseen shape stole through it like a wisp of smoke. The window slid shut again. For a moment, had anyone been in the room, they might have felt an uncomfortable sense of presence. But then curtains drawn over a portal swayed, and the sense of presence was gone from the room.

* * * *

There was a long, narrow hallway that curved its circuit around the base of the glass tower. Thick carpeting lay underfoot, the ceiling was arched and Gothic, from which depended hanging lamps of perforated silver.

Guards were stationed at intervals along the curve of the wall, like statues. Purplish of skin were these, bald and burly, clad in gaudy pantaloons of green and canary and scarlet silk. They were Keshites, he knew, brought thither as slaves from the orchid-perfumed jungles of the Southlands, where rose the bright spires of the Gold City. Alert and awake were they, for their dread master was now in residence; but, for all their vigilance, they saw nor heard naught as the unseen form of the Warlock stole past on soundless feet.

Kellory searched room after room, peering into suites and apartments and inner chambers, as he explored the base of the glass tower. He was in an infernal haste to find the girl Carthalla and begone, for the Gygian spell would not last beyond the hour, and the Ring could not then be reused for a fortnight.

In some of the rooms women languished, some naked, many in chains or one or another form of ingenious bondage. There were slender boys, their nude, ambiguous bodies sprawled languidly on silken sheets, their girlishly pretty features painted like courtesans. There were even small girl-children. All of these were reserved for the Prince's pleasure, and it would seem that the Prince took pleasure in many ways...

Kellory's grim mouth twisted in a sour grimace. Such dainty perversions were unknown to the gaunt, dour, vengeance-driven Warlock; he could not help wondering if such as Prince Parlion were worth saving from the savage Thungoda...

He prowled on, viewless as a gust of breeze.

Then he came to a curtained portal guarded by two stalwart sentinels in gilded cuirasses, greaves, gauntlets and scarlet-plumed helms, with longswords scabbarded at their thighs.

And Kellory surmised that he had reached the object of his quest.

Like a phantom, he glided through the curtains and vanished into the room beyond.

# CHAPTER 9

## STEEL AGAINST SORCERY

Within, all was dim and shadowy. The large and sumptuously decorated room was illuminated by wan lamps of perforated silver which leaked a perfumed vapor.

The floor was buried beneath thick carpets woven to depict fanciful gardens, and it was littered with cozy nests of plump pillows. Low divans stood along the walls, draped in shimmering fabrics.

Kellory spared only a swift, all-encompassing glance at these surroundings—which was, in a way, a pity, for the room was exquisitely and strangely decorated. From a huge urn of red stone, a carved wooden tree grew, its sculpted branches hung with glistening plaques of jade and malachite and smalt-blue enamel, like leaves. Dangling fruit hung from the carven branches by thin gold chains: sleek melons carved from enormous chunks of amber, grape-clusters of blue and purple crystals, fabulous uzolbs crusted with yellow topazes, and flowers of silver covered with twinkling garnets and rubies.

A cage of curved crystal bars held a jeweled mechanical bird whose metal beak uttered a sleepy, warbling song like wind-chimes.

In a wide basin of lucent alabaster, leaped a fountain of liquid light, devised by a magician for the Prince's pleasure.

Tapestries of opal cloth hung against the walls, which were paneled in fruitwoods. The shimmering cloth changed colors in chameleon fashion, and patterns of reflected light shifted magically, as the light cloth moved to every vagrant breath of air.

But Kellory had no time to observe these marvels.

Thick velvet curtains, the colors of peacock plumes, metallic green and indigo and bronze, were drawn over the tall, half-open windows along the farther wall, and one of these was but partly curtained, giving forth a view of luxurious gardens, bathed in the shifting luminance of the colored moons. Iophoon, the Red Moon, stood on the horizon and by its level shafts of ruby light Kellory could make out the scene which lay before him.

Naked, Carthalla writhed in the arms of a slender, effete man with gilt hair and painted eyelids. The girl seemed drugged, her struggles curiously ineffective and languorous. His hands were fondling her body while his painted mouth nuzzled the soft hollow of her throat. One beringed hand stole down from her panting breast to caress her thighs—

Kellory strode forward and smote the painted man with his Staff. The blow, coming as it seemed from empty air, left the pampered princeling stunned. He fell from the low divan on which he had been lolling and thumped to the floor with a gasp in a tangle of bare limbs and disarranged garments.

Kellory wasted no time, for the Gygian spell of invisibility was nearly exhausted, and could not be renewed. He snatched the naked girl to her feet and half-led, half-dragged her to the tall window.

"Ho! Guards—*an assassin!*" shrilled the Prince, staggering to his feet and clutching his raiment about his loins with shaking hands.

Kellory propped Carthalla against the casement and turned, brandishing his Staff. And even in that same moment, the Gygian magic died and his wavering shadowy form melted into being, and slowly took on shape and hue and substance.

The twin sentinels burst into the suite to stare with astonished eyes as a gaunt, wild-eyed man in tight black leather, wrapped in a swirling cloak, came into being out of empty air, like an apparition or a dream.

Green eyes blazing like those of a trapped beast from the tangle of wild witchlocks, white teeth bared in a threatening snarl in the lean, leathery face, Kellory confronted his adversaries and held them for a long moment at bay. Then as the Prince gestured fearfully, the two came at him with bared naked steel flashing in gauntleted fists.

Then the metal-shod Staff stood between them: muttering a Word, Kellory spun the rod, which traced a sputtering half-circle of green fire on the dimness. It hung there, spitting crackling sparks, like an enchanted barrier.

Licking their lips and signing themselves superstitiously, the guards shrank from the circle of fire, glancing uneasily at each other.

"Cut him down, fools!" shrilled the Prince, from the safety of a far corner. The two came warily forward again to face the lean, menacing figure in black. One thrust forth his sword in a lightning-swift stroke, but the bare metal brushed the magic circle of green flame—Light flared! Sparks flew. The guard half-fell to his knees, clutching singed fingers as the red-hot blade fell to sizzle against the thick carpeting.

The other guard fell back warily, refusing to obey the screeched imprecations that spewed from Parlion's painted lips.

"You cannot fight sorcery with steel, Sire," he muttered.

The long moment stretched out, taut and interminable. But Kellory knew the impasse would not last for long; other guards could be heard clumping down the curving corridor towards the pleasure-chambers of the Prince, and soon he would face more adversaries than even he could hold back with his magic fire...

# CHAPTER 10

## THE WEB OF DARKNESS

When the second contingent of guardsmen came into the chamber, they found a lone man holding at bay two of their number, one who sprawled groaning on the floor, nursing his burnt hand, while the other stood with brandished steel, unwilling or unable to charge the Warlock.

With their number joined to him, however, they would be able to rush the lean black sorcerer from all sides at once, one sword-stroke diverting his attention from another. They fell into precise line, like the well-disciplined palace troops they were, and advanced upon Kellory with measured stride.

"Cut the blackguard down," panted Prince Parlion, licking thin lips. "But do not harm the wench!"

The cool night air from the moonlit gardens had partially aroused the Sarkovy girl from her drugged trance-like state; she gradually became aware of her dark companion's predicament, and the deadly danger which encompassed them now on all sides.

"Can you not smite them with magic lightnings, as you slew the Thungoda who had taken me?" she whispered dazedly to Kellory. The Warlock grimly shook his head.

"There are too many of them," he said in cold and level tones. "My powers are still too depleted to strike down such a number. Were my Gygian Ring still imbued with Power, we could both steal from here unobserved, but, alas—"

Suddenly he broke off, as a scheme occurred to him. If the Gygian spell was beyond him, there was, perchance, another of similar nature he could employ—

Shifting his Staff to the grasp of his crippled hand, he fished in his pouchful of periapts, finding by sense of touch alone the amulet he required. It was a triangular bit of black obsidian, whose glittering surface was carefully graven with two mystic runes. Touching it to brow, lips and heart, and reaching down within himself to the sources of Power, he uttered a Word at whose potent syllables the walls groaned and the flooring shuddered.

Darkness fell!

Pitch-black it was, an inky night unbroken by even the faintest luminance, an unrelieved gloom such as that which must reign at the bottom of the deepest sea.

Like men suddenly stricken stone-blind, the guards stumbled, tripped over pillows, fell in a clash of metal, crying out in sharp alarm.

"I—am—*blind!*" screamed the Prince, clutching at his distorted face, clawing with gilded nails at his wide, unseeing eyes. Shrieking hysterically, he blundered from the room into the corridor beyond, where blackness lay as in his chamber.

"What—what is the matter with them?" gasped Carthalla in frightened tones, as Kellory scooped her up in strong lean arms and shoved her through the half-curtained, open window, following after. They dropped lightly to the smooth, emerald turf below.

"It is called the Web of Darkness," he said tersely, "a spell that negates all visible light. They are as men suddenly struck blind—not only can they see us not, but the terror of being blind overwhelms their bravery."

"How, then, can *we* see?" faltered the girl. "For I can see everything as clearly as before."

Kellory showed her the talisman of black volcanic glass he clutched in his one good hand.

"While I hold this, and you are near me, we alone are free of the Web of Darkness, which obscures the light from all others. Come—let us begone from this place of cold perversions swiftly!" He led her off through the gardens which dreamed languidly under the floating moons.

The ring of sentinels had crumbled when the spell of darkness overwhelmed their sight. Now they wandered about, stumbling into unseen obstacles, weeping and calling out. Through the lines of the watch they passed with ease, avoiding the groping figures who could not see them in the depths of their blindness.

"I left my pony tethered in those trees," Kellory whispered. "We shall have to share the saddle, for I procured only one steed, such was my haste."

They untied the pony, which nuzzled Kellory's shoulder gratefully, free of its fear at blindness upon the instant of his touch. They mounted and headed for the river, where an arched bridge spanned the gliding silvery floods.

None saw them pass from the palace grounds; none saw them ride across the bridge to the farther shore of the river.

"You seem always to be rescuing me from some peril or another," murmured the girl, resting wearily in the strong circle of Kellory's arms.

"And you seem to be always getting yourself into trouble," he remarked sarcastically. The girl bridled a little at his harsh words.

"How was I to know the furtive little man watching us in the aleroom was one of the Prince's panders?" she demanded.

Kellory shrugged wordlessly.

They rode on in silence.

# CHAPTER 11

## THE PLACE CALLED OMBOR

Across the river, they took the long road north and rode under the many-colored moons without further conversation. Once well beyond the chances of pursuit, Kellory relaxed and then cancelled the spell of darkness, for to maintain it further seemed pointless and he wished to conserve his strength against the possibility of future needs.

The legion had marched this way, for the meadow-grass beyond the margin of the road was trampled as if under the feet of many marching men, and wagon wheels or chariot wheels had cut deep grooves in the soil where it was barren of grass. Kellory briefly explained to Carthalla his desire to join forces with the Duke against the Thungoda.

"Will he accept aid from a magician?" the girl questioned in dubious tones. "In these parts, men tend to distrust the works of wizards, and often drive them hence with stones…"

Kellory shrugged. "Time will tell us that," he remarked.

They rode on, making all possible speed. The pony was fresh enough, and had rested during Kellory's adventures in the Prince's villa, but the double load was doubtless tiring to the beast and Kellory feared it would be daybreak before they caught up with Almery's troop.

The two riders were wearied from their exertions, as well. After a time, Carthalla dozed in the shelter of the Warlock's arms, wrapped in his black cloak.

* * * *

It was even as Kellory had thought: the day lacked of an hour before the rising of Kylix the sun-star, when they came within sight of the rear-guard of the legion, and were soon halted by outriders who questioned them closely. At Kellory's insistence, they escorted the two to the head of the legion, where Duke Almery received them on a knoll with his officers.

"Well, Warlock, I see that you came, after all," cried the Duke heartily, with a curious glance of his candid gray eyes at the girl, naked under the black cloak. "And it seems that you carried off a bit of booty from Novodny city to comfort you in the wars!"

Kellory did not smile, and tersely explained Carthalla's presence, giving a brief account of her rescue from under the very nose of the Prince. The Duke stared, then laughed.

"A good thing for us all that I have given up hopes of help from *that* source," he boomed, "otherwise your rude theft of the new harem favorite would have aroused the ire of Parlion, in truth!"

The Duke gave Carthalla a pony to ride, and clothing with which to cover her nakedness. Shortly thereafter, they mounted and rode on, with Almery graciously offering Kellory a place at the head of the legion. He seemed intrigued by the grim, tight-lipped Warlock, and curious about his past, his motives and what powers he could employ against their common enemy. And he drew from Kellory every scrap of information he possessed about the Thungoda and the modes of waging war.

In the middle of conversation, quite suddenly, the Warlock halted his steed and sat the saddle, staring to his left. Puzzled, the Duke followed the direction of his gaze, but saw nothing more startling than a level knoll, like a miniature plateau, littered with rubble and broken stones.

"What is this place?" demanded Kellory.

The Duke briefly passed the query along to one of his aides, a cartographer, who rustled through his bag of maps, coming up with a name.

"It is called Ombor, my Lord," the fellow said. Almery passed the information along to the Warlock; then his slight frown of puzzlement cleared from his brow as he recognized the name.

"Was it not hereabouts that your party of wizards long ago paused before turning back to Novodny city?" he murmured.

Kellory nodded, his tense face alive with an excitement which even Carthalla had never before seen in that taciturn visage.

"It is," he said.

Then he tugged his pony's head about, and cantered up the slope to the crest of the flat knoll.

# CHAPTER 12

## THE SECRET OF THE BEAST

The crest of the knoll had been artificially leveled at some time in the ancient ages of the past, and once a structure of hewn stone had stood here. But now it stood no more. The years had toppled the stone building long ago, and now it lay in tumbled, broken fragments of worn stone, green and rust-colored from mold and lichen, crumbling away under the tireless erosion of wind and weather. But it could still be seen, if only by the foundations, that the knoll had once held a square stone building, perhaps a temple or a shrine.

It was not these fallen blocks of stone that held interest for Kellory; indeed, he barely gave them a passing glance as he guided his sure-footed steed through the broken piles of rubble to where the one thing stood that had caught his attention from the road below. He halted before it and dismounted, and stood regarding it in deep thought for a time, arms folded upon his breast, while the Duke and Carthalla approached, dismounted and came up to him with open curiosity in their faces.

The thing that Kellory had seen from the road was the tallest of the stones wherewith the crest of the knoll was littered, and it alone was not broken nor had it fallen from its place. Once it had stood before the portal of the shrine, no doubt, based upon the stone pave whose surviving shards could still be glimpsed between ragged weeds and scruffy patches of grass and green beds of moss.

It was a monolith, a great mass of gray stone sparkling with veins of bright mica that glinted in the light of the sun-star. And it had once been hewn in the likeness of a crouching beast, a mythical thing with the haunches of a pony, the forelimbs of a predatory bird, and the face of a bearded man. True, the centuries, as they passed, had effaced the clear lines of the stone beast with their careless hands, rounding and smoothing away the sculptor's work until little more was left than a huge shapeless boulder, in which it required considerable imagination to recognize it as the work of man. But it was.

"The Ghaast," said Kellory tonelessly. And indeed it was.

Carthalla touched her lips with her fingers, wonderingly. But Almery looked puzzled, staring dubiously at the wind-worn, but still faintly recognizable, features of the man-headed beast.

"A creature of heraldry, is't not?" Almery asked. Kellory shook his head.

"Of myth. The Guardian of Secrets, the Enjoiner to Silence. Of old, a stone Ghaast crouched before the portal of each temple or shrine, and guarded the entryway to the Mysteries."

They stepped nearer, staring up into the stone face which stared out over their heads at the level plains and the distant city, and the misty horizon. Like a man's face it was, bearded, the hair arranged in an antique style, the eyes calm, wise and unreadable. Upon the slightly parted lips of the stone image was a cryptic and mysterious smile.

Kellory stepped forward and mounted the crumbling base of the statue. Reaching up, he inserted his left hand into the open, smiling lips of worn stone.

The day was bright, and hot, and still. The clouds hung motionless against the blue of heaven, as if painted there. Hunting-hawks hovered high against the blaze of light. No wind rustled through the bushes that had sprung up between the fallen stones of the ancient temple. It was as if all of Nature held its breath in suspense, as Kellory searched within the mouth-cavity of the stony beast.

His searching fingers found dirt and rock-dust and dry leaves and an old spiderweb.

Then they closed upon a metal box.

He drew it carefully forth; it was old, the bright metal tarnished green with verdigris.

He opened the latch. Within lay a flat object tightly wrapped in stout leather. Once that leather had been oiled, or perhaps dipped in wax; now it was dry and crumbling into flakes beneath the touch of Kellory's fingers.

He peeled away the leather coverings and cast them aside.

He held in his hands a thin book, bound in carved boards of black wood.

He opened it carefully, scanning the contents, almost holding his breath.

The pages—there were only fourteen of them in all—were of thick, excellent parchment, relatively untouched by time, although the crabbed characters wherewith each page was covered were not easily legible, their inks having faded through the passage of years. But they could still be read with study, those pages.

Lifting his head, he stared past his friends off across the plain, remembering...

> ...And they carried hither with them into Sarkovy the Book of Yaohim the Wise, the which now lieth hidden behind the smile of the Ghaast.

He had found the Book of Shadows, and his quest was ended. And the hour of his vengeance, long delayed, was nigh to hand.

# PART 6

## LORD OF THE SHADOWS

# CHAPTER 1

## AGAINST THE NIGHT

Into the great central plains of Sarkovy there moved a mighty host of armed men. Foot soldiers trudged through the long grasses, pikes aslant over their shoulders, torsos clad in leather jerkins now stained with road-dust. Officers in rich cloaks of maroon, canary, cobalt blue, went cantering by on their shaggy, horned ponies. In the rear, lumbering bouphonts dragged heavily laden wains filled with wargear, baggage and tenting.

At the head of the legion rode its commander, the great Duke, a bold, laughing, huge golden bear of a man in gilt byrnie and burnished cuirass, his plumed helm doffed so that the breeze combed through his thick blond curls. Near his position rode two strangers, obviously newcomers to the host. There was a lean, dark man in black leather, with a somber, brooding face, and a bright-haired Sarkovy girl, his companion.

These were Kellory the Warlock and Carthalla of Khev, only daughter of the High Prince of Khev.

For many days the legion had trudged up the broad north road, on their way to the meadowlands called the Borgatyr Plain, where in their numberless thousands the Thungoda hordesmen were reputed to be encamped below the gates of Grand Khev.

Over the heads of the marching men floated a bright banner of royal purple, charged with a fabulous beast with snarling jaws open to reveal its triple rows of triangular shark-like teeth, its man-face framed in the spiky mane of a great jungle cat. This was the Mantichore, the emblem of Duke Almery's ancient house. The symbol was known and respected and even feared for many leagues about the southern city of Novodny, from which the legion had marched; even here in the North it was not unknown, and it was curious that so huge a force of warriors could enter the central plains about Grand Khev without being halted or queried by knights of that city. But every frontier garrison they passed, and every fort guarding a river-ford or bridge, was empty of men for some mysterious and troubling reason.

To leave a garrison unmanned, to abandon a fort, the gates open to any intruder, was not only contrary to the traditions of war, it went against common sense. And Duke Almery and his men were puzzled by this ominous and inexplicable fact. Therefore, they pressed on into the North with all possible speed, anxious to gain the environs of Khev and confer with the Prince of that city, the lord Valemyr.

At measured intervals of time, the legion made temporary halt to rest and refresh themselves, for armies march no faster than the weariest yeoman, and tired men make poor warriors. During such times, while Carthalla joined the Duke and his officers at wine and cheese and meat, Kellory brooded alone, poring over the crabbed letters of an old book. He had spent many years of his life in questing for this volume, the legended Grimoire of Yaohim the Wise, and it required much study for him to puzzle his way through its quaint, antique charactery.

But the secrets locked in the few pages this thin book contained were of more might than all this great legion of armed men. And time was running short: he must master the secret of the Book of Shadows ere they faced the Horde in war, or all the long years of his searching would have been wasted in vain.

"I wonder of what use the magic in that old book will be to him," mused the Duke, toying with a wine goblet of chased gold. "Or to us, when it is out sword—strike and slay!—and devils take all this idle magicking!"

Carthalla did not know the answer to that question, so she shrugged wordlessly.

"Still and all, my Lord Duke," said one of the senior officers, a man named Emoric, "if the Thungoda-shamans strive to wreak spells against us, 'tis wise to have a Warlock on our side of the battle." The Duke nodded thoughtfully and emptied his cup.

"I have seen his magic many times," confided the blond girl. "It is very powerful, but limited. To use it taxes his strength fearfully, and then he must rest and renew his Power before he may freely use it again."

"How many men have you known him to wield his magic against at one time?" inquired the Duke. Carthalla thought back to their first meeting, there at the crest of the Arul Pass, when the dark man had rescued her from the Thungoda war party.

"Nine," she said hesitantly.

The Duke stared and swore.

*"Nine?"* he repeated incredulously. "But if mine scouts and spies report accurately, we shall face ten thousand of the Thungoda upon the Plain of Borgatyr! This many, it is believed, lie there encamped already,

with thousands more filtering down from Barbaria into the South daily—"

Carthalla spread her slim, strong hands placatingly.

"I only know this, that Kellory believes the spells in the Book of Shadows will enable him to crush them in all their thousands, as once the great Yaohim destroyed the Sea Devils with that same identical spell," she said. The Duke looked skeptical.

"If he can unriddle the cantrips of the Book in time," said Almery.

Carthalla avoided his eyes. She knew that he was right, and it seemed—even to her—that all the magic secrets in the world could hardly be enough to whelm and crush the numberless thousands of the savage Thungoda...

And if they were not crushed, the howling savages would trample down the bright cities of Sarkovy, bringing the black night of Barbaria down across the world. It was to strive against the night that they were come hither, Kellory and Carthalla. But with what hope of victory?

# CHAPTER 2

## POWERS OF EARTH

Along towards twilight, the legion camped at a place marked on the maps as the Vale of Druga. While the yeomen erected tents for the night and cooks lit their fires, the officers let their ponies graze the lush meadowgrass and gathered for the evening council at the tent of their commander.

"Captain Uthric, I will give your company the honor of guarding our rest this night," said the Duke. "Post your sentries and mount the watch as soon as our steeds are penned."

"Yes, my lord."

The Duke turned to another officer, the chief of his scouts, a lean and grizzled man of indeterminate years named Andreth.

"I am uneasy at the absence of men in these parts," he said. "Surely there should be a travelers' inn at the ford of that river yonder, and a smithy. Take your Rangers and investigate."

"Aye," said the older man shortly, with a sketchy salute. He turned and strode off to where his men waited, crouched on their hunkers. They were a lean and rangy, long-limbed crew, with bronzed, leathery faces and clear eyes like hawks. Kellory liked the looks of them, whereas he felt less than comfortable with the stolid yeomen, the proud officers, the mounted knights. Some inner prompting made him volunteer to go out with them: even he could not have explained the urge.

They fanned out on foot, gliding through the bushes that fringed the edges of the river. Here some of the ponies of the legion still drank, silky muzzles buried to the nostrils in the cold, foaming water. Pale green reeds and brown rushes bent to the evening breeze. All was cool and calm in the lengthening shadows. All was peaceful and still.

Why, then, did Kellory feel the invisible brush of fear against his nerve-endings, the chill touch of foreboding up his spine?

He stared around, frowning. There was an inn, aye, and a smithy, too, on the far side of the ford; or, rather, there had once been. For now only the blackened husks of burnt-out buildings stood knee-deep in thick grass.

Andreth led his Rangers across the ford, where muddy humps stood above the shallow waters. And, all at once, Kellory stretched out his good hand in an involuntary gesture of warning and a cry rose unbidden to his lips—"Watch out!"

On the far side of the river the first few men were wading ashore. There the earth lay bare beside the river, a wallow of greasy brown mud and stagnant water. Even as Kellory shouted his warning, the wet earth uncannily rose, twisting and molding itself like a great mass of soft clay in the fingers of an invisible hand—A great lumpy mass of brown mud rose up, slapped about one of the foremost of the Rangers, who stood fear-frozen, slack-jawed in astonishment.

The man gave voice to a muffled scream before the muddy mass swallowed him up.

Andreth swore, whipping out his long dirk from the scabbard strapped to one lean thigh. He sprang forward and attacked the mud-mass, but his keen blade met no resistance, merely slicing off a soggy layer of matter, which flopped to the ground.

Another sprang to his aid. They dug both hands into the heaving mound of muck, dragged their comrade free of the uncanny thing that had swallowed him up; and bore him a safe distance away.

"Dead," muttered the man beside Andreth. His chief looked sick.

"Drowned alive in mud," he growled. "A horrible way to die!"

Kellory forded the stream, every sense alert, his long Staff in his hand. But even as his feet touched the farther shore, the mudhill slumped, sagged, slid back into the hollow from which it had molded itself. He ran to join the Rangers who stood about their chief, who still knelt above the dead man.

"Get away from this place," Kellory snapped, for they knelt on bare muddy earth. But in the same breath the mud beneath their very feet humped, rose, scattering the men to every side. Andreth jumped to his feet, cursing, as his men withdrew—all but the one who had helped him retrieve the corpse of the first man taken.

A huge section of fluid mud extruded itself from the heaving flanks of the thing. It arched out, slapped about the middle of the startled man, who yelled and dug his own blade into the doughy stuff, flailing out with his other arm.

Kellory grabbed his hand—tugged. The man came loose from the loathsome embrace of the sucking mud with some difficulty. They dragged him into the grass where the other men stood.

"What is it?" whispered Andreth to Kellory.

"An *unggog,*" the Warlock said crisply. "An earth-elemental, roused to sentience long ago, perhaps, by some grim sorcery."

"No wonder this place is deserted," muttered Andreth apprehensively. Kellory nodded.

"They burned the inn and the forge, hoping to drive it away," he mused. "Fire is traditionally the foe of earth, as water is of wind."

"Well, it didn't work," said Andreth. "How do we fight it? For unless the legion takes this crossing-place, we must trudge many weary leagues to the next ford—"

"We don't fight it," said Kellory in dull, heavy tones. "It cannot be fought. It has the very strength of the earth itself..."

# CHAPTER 3

## THE BEAST OF DRUGA

The Rangers squatted on their hams, safe amidst the grasses. For Kellory explained that only when they were on the bare earth, which was wet and plastic and could be molded into shape by the invisible power of the elemental, were they in any danger. But even he was not too certain.

They stared at the placid stretch of mud, now innocently flat again, for the humped thing had collapsed again. They did not know what to do. This was the first time any of them, save only for Kellory, had faced a foe that could not feel the cold kiss of their steel, and it roused superstitious dread within their breasts.

Kellory alone stood, brooding, arms folded upon his chest, regarding the mudflats thoughtfully. He had never fought an earth-elemental before and was unsure what to do.

Andreth returned to the camp to report the emergency to the Duke, leaving his lieutenant, Osgir, in charge. This was the man Kellory had pulled free of the embrace of the mud-monster. Soon the Duke and his guards and Carthalla came to observe the marvel and to confer.

"All is quiet enough now," boomed the Duke in his hearty tones. Andreth grunted and spat.

"Things were lively enough a little while ago," he said, indicating the muddy corpse of the man the elemental had slain. The Duke regarded it soberly. Then he turned to Kellory.

"Well, Master Kellory, you are the wizard here, not I—what shall we do? I command in battle, siege or foray; but when it comes to witchery, I am as useless as the greenest recruit. How do we put down this murderous menace?"

"I—don't know," admitted Kellory. And he explained the vast strength of the mud-monster, and how, by its very nature, it was unkillable.

"It is naught but a spirit, invisible and impalpable, but able to mold the substance of earth into form and to give it motion. It cannot be slain with steel."

"I can testify to that, my lord," said Andreth. And he told how their blades had merely cut away portions of the soft earth without causing the thing discomfort. The Duke made a troubled frown.

"Well, we could go on to the next ford, albeit it lies many days' march away. The ford here at Druga is more convenient, of course... and time is the heart of the problem. For aught we know the Thungoda are battering at the very gates of Khev at this moment. If we march to the next ford, we may arrive to find the city a heap of soot-black rubble, and the Thungoda on the march. Have you nothing to suggest, Master Kellory?"

"Post sentinels on both sides of the river," suggested the Warlock. "Plant torches in the earth to light the mudflats so we can observe it if it stirs again. And let me think..."

Duke Almery shrugged, but did as Kellory said. Night had fallen by now, and the moons of Zephrondus had not yet uprisen over the edges of the world.

The evening meal had been by now prepared. They at the ford ate from tin dishes, attentive of the least stirrings in the mud. Kellory alone did not feel hungry; he brooded sullenly atop a low hillock, striving to remember the lore of elemental beings he had learned from his master, the Green Enchanter.

There was little enough known of the creatures, he realized. Seldom did they manifest themselves upon the surface of the world, and this was especially true of earth-elementals, who resided deep in the cavernous bowels of the planet—if a bodiless spirit can be said to "reside" any-where, that is.

Once, early in the days he had shared with Carthalla, the Warlock had faced and fought a *shioggua*, a water-elemental. The creature had inhabited the Black River, he recalled. It had not been an easy thing to drive down the Beast of Black River...and the Beast of Druga would be even harder to fight.

# CHAPTER 4

## SCORCHED EARTH

Time passed. Overhead, the constellations wheeled through the heavens. It came to be the hour of moonrise. Erelong, the skies flushed with pale green fire, signaling the coming-forth of the moon Diostrion. Still Kellory brooded over his somber thoughts.

The Duke became restive. "Have you arrived at some solution to the problem?" he asked. "For we must either put down the demon or march leagues out of our way, and 'twere best we begin the journey, if march we must."

Kellory looked grim. "I have. Withdraw all of your men to the safe side of the river, but leave the torches burning."

"What are you going to do?" whispered Carthalla. He shrugged gloomily.

"I said that an intrinsic conflict exists between the forces of the elements, that they are irreconcilably opposed to each other, wind to water, earth to fire."

She nodded. "I remember! Then—?"

"I will summon a fire elemental, hoping thereby to drive away the earth-spirit," he said briefly.

The Duke looked dubiously at the Warlock. "Will it work? Is there any danger to men?"

"There is always a danger to men when spirits war," Kellory said heavily. "But with running water between your men and the elemental spirits, they should be safe enough. Spirits of fire dislike crossing streams."

"And—?"

"They are not hard to call up," said the Warlock. "But they are hard to keep under control. It is the nature of fire to be mischievous, capricious, unreliable. And they are even harder to force back down, once summoned."

Duke Almery shivered a little, but went about the issuing of commands. The Rangers withdrew to the farther side of the river, leaving the mudflat ringed about with burning torches. Kellory searched the sky with keen eyes, noting the position of certain stars and planets, awaiting a favorable configuration of the heavens.

Then he began.

The charms he muttered under his breath were in a language unknown to his auditors; the signs he traced upon the night air with his wizardly Staff likewise meant nothing to them. But somewhere—Something—heard.

It did not respond.

Kellory performed the ritual again. This time, the sweat gleamed on his brows and lean cheeks and beaded his upper lip. They could sense the strain in him, like the strings of a musical instrument stretched taut, tauter still, nigh to the breaking point. Carthalla had seen this before, and knew that the Warlock was striving to impose the force of his trained will upon the pattern of natural forces that sustain the planet.

"The *shiarra* resists me," he muttered between stiff lips. "I must try again…"

"Look!" said the Duke, pointing. Across the river, the earth-elemental seemingly sensed the summoning of its rival: slick mud humped high, shaping itself into a towering, viscous pillar. The soldiers whispered the names of their gods, fingered amulets and talismans. Kellory repeated the ceremony a third time with all the power of his will behind every potent syllable and gesture.

Suddenly the fire-elemental responded! The flame of the torches which ringed the mudflats burned an eerie blue, then a virulent and unnatural green—then blinding white!

The torches exploded into fountains of fire. The fire-jets crumbled into clouds of blazing sparks. It was as if all of the fireflies in the world had gathered suddenly in one place: an uncanny sight.

The soldiers stared, the whites of their wide eyes clearly visible in the flickering murk.

"Look at him now!" muttered Almery to the girl. She looked.

Wrapped in his black cloak, Kellory stood like a graven image atop a hillock, confronting the force he had called up. Dark and lean and tall, his motionless figure stood, and it seemed to their eyes that he was taller than a mortal man, like a soaring pillar of black iron. In the darkness which cloaked him, his green eyes flared like emerald moons, as bright or brighter than the Emerald Moon above their heads.

The fire-flecks swirled about into a spinning vortex, then a wheel of glittering motes of light which revolved rapidly. A hissing sound came to their ears, the sound made by the fire-sparks as they cut through the cool air.

From the whirling fire-wheel, a whip of scintillant flame snapped out, to lash about the glistening pile of quivering mud. Moisture whiffed into steam. Mud sizzled. Underfoot, the earth trembled, heaved, groaned, as if in pain.

A great slab of mud sloughed away, slapping at the fire-whip as a man slaps at an annoying fly.

The fire-whip parted, but rejoined instantly. Now it was burning its way through the wet, quaking mass, cutting the tower of mud in two halves.

A distant bellowing came from underfoot. The earth shook, feathery trees whipping as if to the force of an unseen wind.

More sparks flew from the whirling wheel to feed the strength of the noose which tightened about the decomposing column. It had bitten now through the mud, and the column was falling apart. The portion severed by the noose of fire exploded into flying clods of dried earth.

"*Look*," groaned the Duke through numb lips.

When the upper half of the mud-pile exploded, it left behind a stain on the air like a dark cloud of vapor. This roiled and seethed uncertainly—then congealed as the fire-wheel broke up and hurled darts of flame into the cloudy darkness.

The earth gave one last surge, then was still. Steam hissed from the burnt stretch of dry mud, from which all moisture was gone. Gone, too, was the dark stain on the night air.

Kellory sagged, steadying himself with his Staff.

"Go back down, *shiarra*," he whispered, bending the glare of his green eyes on the cloud of fire-sparks, which now drifted about aimlessly hither and yon.

One by one, the sparks died. The fire-cloud was gone; gone, as well, was the huge force which had inhabited the mud-slick.

They helped the exhausted Warlock down and gave him cold wine to drink.

"The land is cleansed now and safe for men," he said hoarsely.

"We will cross the ford at once," decided the Duke. Turning to his officers, he said, "Summon your companies and get them into order. I want to put a good, healthy distance between this place and ourselves before the rising of the second moon."

# CHAPTER 5

## KELLORY DEPARTS

For the next two days the legion marched deeper into the North, encountering neither resistance nor welcome. All of the land seemed to be deserted by men, the farmhouses vacant, the inns empty and abandoned. It was as if Grand Khev had called in every man, either for their protection or its defense.

Duke Almery did not like the notion.

"It looks as though the Thungoda have moved against the city of your royal father," he said to Carthalla one evening as they sat in his tent, sharing wine.

"How soon will we know if your suspicions are true?" asked the girl. He shrugged.

"I have dispatched my scouts, mounted on the swiftest ponies," he said. "When they return, we will know. I pray to the gods we will arrive in time to relieve the city, if it lies under siege."

"You have only one legion," she observed. "Will it be enough to turn the tide of war against the Thungoda? Kellory believes they have mustered many thousands. I have told you the number of my father's troops: will your strength, added to his own, suffice to drive back the Hordesmen?"

"No," said the Duke quietly. He did not look at her as he spoke the word.

They said no more, for there was nothing more to be said. But Carthalla knew that if the Thungoda were not stopped at the gates of Khev, they would move south, destroying each of the Seven Cities in turn, until at last all of the lush, green land of Sarkovy was a wilderness inhabited only by corpses.

It was an ugly thought.

Kellory had absented himself from these conversations, as he had from the Duke's councils. Every available moment he spent poring over the closely written pages of the Book of Shadows, striving to master its arcane lore. Time was running out, he knew, and a half-mastered spell is no spell at all.

He avoided converse with Almery and with Carthalla. Nor did he seem to eat or sleep. Nightly, candles burnt till dawn behind the dark tent in which he had chosen to immure himself. When they saw him for the morning's march, he seemed drawn and haggard, his face gaunt and lined, his shoulders stooped with fatigue. But he refused to listen when Carthalla begged him to eat and rest.

"He drives himself more mercilessly than you drive your soldiers," she complained to Almery. "He will kill himself if he does not rest."

The Duke favored her with a tired smile.

"As for that, my lady, we will all be dead soon enough, if your Warlock does not master the task to which he has set himself," he said dryly. She said no more.

\* \* \* \*

Towards evening of that day the scouts returned, ponies lathered and staggering with fatigue. The riders flung themselves from the saddles, to report that all was even as the Duke had feared: Grand Khev had been under Thungoda siege for more than six days, and the walls had been breached in half a dozen places.

"There is fighting in the streets," reported one of the men, "and we could see the smoke of burning buildings. It is only a matter of time before the city falls to the savages."

"Has Prince Valemyr yet taken the field against them?" inquired the Duke. His men shook their heads.

"It would seem the Prince is holding back from that final measure until all is clearly lost," said the scout. "His force, as we judge, is too small to make very much difference, after all. But it is the only hope he has, since he knows naught of your coming, lord."

The Duke gnawed on his nether lip, striding back and forth restively. Then he turned to dispatch a page, summoning his captains.

"See that your men are fed and given strong wine, and have an hour's rest," he commanded. "Tonight we will march, rather than sleep, for by tomorrow we may be too late to help."

Then he turned to the Warlock and Carthalla.

"My lady, Master Kellory, I regret cutting short your badly needed rest, but time is the matter here—"

Kellory did not change his somber expression. "In any event, Lord Duke, I part company with you here," he said shortly. The Duke stared at him.

"You are not going with us to Grand Khev—?"

"I will be there before you," said the Warlock.

Almery opened his mouth to ask how, then closed it on the words. Wizards had ways other men could not know, he realized.

By moonrise, Kellory had vanished.

They began the last leg of their long march, praying that they would be in time to aid the Khevya.

# CHAPTER 6

## AT THE GATES OF KHEV

As the moons rose up over the edges of the world, the Prince of Grand Khev stood on a hilltop, marshalling his few remaining knights and yeomen for one last stand against the Thungoda.

Already, the city itself was invested by the Hordesmen. The black smoke of burning palaces stained the clean night air; moonslight gleamed on the broken wall of the city, where siege-engines had riven a rude path through the smooth stone.

In his gilded armor, wrapped in a fluttering cloak of fine scarlet, the Prince of Khev made a brave sight. But inwardly he was bone-weary and heartsick. In the months that had passed since his only daughter had been taken by Thungoda raiders on the road to easterly Aijan, matters had gone from bad to worse. For a time, the Thungoda had played with embassies and conciliatory discussions; now, much too late, he bitterly realized that the bandy-legged little savages had only been stalling for time to permit more of their forces to descend out of the frozen North. And also they had awaited the coming of their dread warlord, Prince Mnar, to come hither from his dark throne in the City of Terror.

Things had indeed gone from bad to worse, thought the Prince of Khev to himself. And now they could hardly worsen more. Even death would be a blessing, in that it would make an end to the fighting and the slaughter of his nobles, and the suffering of the women.

Before him, on the grassy plain before the gates of burning Khev, the *mengli* or encampment of the Horde stretched like a town of tents, enormous under the lambent moons. As yet, they had not come up against him and his surviving force, even when they rode forth from burning Khev to challenge the might of the Thungoda. It was almost as if they disdained so easy a victory! And, in truth, their victory would be an easy one, he grimly knew, for the small force of warriors ringed about him would not for very long stand in the path of the Thungoda in all their thousands.

It was a grim task to stand helplessly by and look on as idle spectators as palaces and temples were plundered and gutted and given over to the flames. Almost was he tempted to sound the charge now, without waiting for the clear light of dawn—to risk all on a final assault—to drive his knights against the broken walls of his own city—anything, to make an end to the waiting!

His gauntleted hand tightened on the gemmed hilt of his sword; almost, he turned to give the signal to his bugler. But even as the thought went through him, a sentry called out in a startled voice and the Prince turned to see a strange sight. Toiling up the slope under guard there approached a man whom he had never before looked upon. The stranger was clad in black leather, his lean form gaunt and emaciated, his face a grim dark mask, his hair a dusty tangle of witchlocks through which green eyes burned with terrible purpose.

"Prince Valemyr?" this scarecrow croaked wearily. The Prince looked him up and down.

"I am he," he admitted wonderingly. "And if you have come to join us against our foe, we are glad of your folly. But I see you bear no sword...?"

"I am a Warlock, no warrior," said the gaunt man. "But I am truly come to lend my strength to yours."

"Then you are welcome amongst us, sir," said the Prince with courteous dignity. "Although I fear you will ride to your death with us, yet will we be proud of your companionship on that last ride..."

"It may not be your last, Lord Prince," replied Kellory. "I bear a weapon so terrible that no other will be needed to rout the Thungoda."

"Indeed, sir? And where is this weapon, pray?"

Kellory gave him the ghost of a grin. With black-gloved fingertips he touched his heart and his brow.

"Here," he said, "and here."

The Prince regarded him coldly. "This is no occasion for jesting, sir."

"I do not jest," said Kellory with equal coldness. "As your lady daughter will inform you, when she arrives—"

Hope flared in the Prince's eyes. "My daughter, sir? What know you of the Princess Carthalla—she yet lives?"

"She lives, and is well," Kellory said. "Together with a legion of the Duke Almery of Novodny, she is only a few hours' march away."

"Then help is on the way, at last!" cried the Prince. "And my child lives...but tell me, sir, how these things came to pass—"

"There is no time for words now," said Kellory with a tired smile. "The time has come for...the Song." The Prince regarded him puzzledly.

Before he could speak, Kellory gestured away the words. "All will soon become clear to you, Lord Prince. For now, let me caution you that what I am about to do is very dangerous. Inform your warriors to avert their eyes from the city of Khev, that your sight be not blasted forever and your hearts shriveled by madness."

The Prince stared at him. There was something in his mien, this grim man with the witch-green eyes, that commanded respect, even awe. He was not a man to boast idly, to spout vain words.

"Vengeance has come at last," breathed Kellory.

And he descended the hill and walked slowly in the direction of the Thungoda encampment...

# CHAPTER 7

## THE SINGING

About the perimeter of the town of tents, the Thungoda had posted their sentries. These leaned upon their hooked spears, yawning and scratching lazily, wishing they could be relieved so as to join their comrades in the plundering of Grand Khev. From time to time, one of the sentries glanced uncaringly at the knoll where the last defenders of Khev had made their stand.

Now one of these straightened, blinked, nudged a companion.

Towards the *mengli* a tall, gaunt figure in black leather came striding. As he walked, he...sang.

They watched the lone man curiously, but with indifference. He was alone and unarmed, and in their fur and iron, in their armed numbers, they feared him not. But they were curious.

For he seemed as unafraid of them as they were of him.

Now the sound of the Song reached their ears. The tune was uncouth, the words unfamiliar. But something about the Song sent a chill crawling up their spines.

He came nearer, his gaze averted from them, staring ahead as if upon nothingness.

They watched him come towards them, leaning idly on their spears, and one of them made a crude jest, something to the effect of, "Behold the lamb comes walking into the very jaws of the wolfpack."

Then they started, muttering. They stared.

For in the gloom of night, Shadows stirred.

Darker they were than the shades cast by men at noontide. They floated up from the earth like wisps of black vapor, like films of impalpable darkness. They clustered at the heels of the tall man as he came walking.

They looked sidewise at one another uneasily, the Thungoda; some murmured superstitiously and wet dry lips with tongue-tip. For no apparent reason, fear grew in their hearts.

One of them snarled a challenge as the gaunt man in black leather approached. He made no reply, neither did he look at them. He strolled through their lines as if they were not there.

As he walked between them, the Shadow-pack broke. Shade by shade, they glided to where the sentinels stood, shifting fearfully from foot to foot, hefting bright steel. The Thungoda eyed the Shadows, fingering the hilts of their weapons. But—how could cold metal bite on nothingness, on empty air?

The Shadows drifted near the Thungoda.

They…*whispered.*

Thin and cold were their voices, like distant echoes. But the Thungoda heard. They shrank, cowered, stumbled away. Some gibbered, clawing at the air, others giggled inanely. One, his face pale as wax, his eyes wide with madness, fell to his knees and began to gnaw the trampled earth.

Another turned his blade against his own belly and died where he had stood, writhing in slow death-pangs like a reptile.

Others broke and ran. But the Shadows followed, gliding effortlessly. Whispering—whispering! With faint, dry voices like the breeze rustling through crisp, dead leaves.

Kellory walked on, his face set like stone. He did not look to either side of him. He did not see the madness, the panic, the death he spread as he walked. He did not hear the whispering or the screams, nor even the strange words of his own Song, for his ears were sealed with wads of wax and his bleak gaze was fixed on nothing.

Now he was among the tents, where Thungoda loafed, drank, gambled, slept. They came to their feet wonderingly; but then the Shadows were beside them, speaking in low, thin voices that which only they could hear.

In their dozens, in their hundreds, the Thungoda fled or fell. Kellory, without breaking his stride, stepped over one mewling warrior who was chewing on his own gory hands. Thungoda turned on Thungoda, striking out with sharp steel. Others turned their knives upon themselves. Some simply squatted and died without seeming cause.

From out of the bowels of the earth, more Shadows rose. They drifted about, each claiming a victim, then another, and another. And the Thungoda shrieked, laughed madly, sobbed, died…

What was it that the Shadows whispered to the men of the Horde? Were they the ghosts of those the warriors had murdered? Did they remind their murderers of intolerable acts, or unmentionable sins? Or did they warn of the unspeakable torments which awaited their miserable spirits beyond the grave, in the dark kingdom of Pnom?

No one can say. And if the answer was written in the Book of Shadows, where Kellory had learned his Song, the Warlock said naught of it to any man, then or later.

But the Thungoda fled, went mad, died laughing horribly, sobbing piteously. And Kellory heeded them not.

* * * *

Into the center of the vast *mengli* he strode, like a grim avenger out of ancient myth. And ever at his heels scuttled the growing host of Shadows. More floated from the earth at every step, the gliding Shadows, the whispering Shadows. And wherever they drifted, men went mad and died. In their hundreds, in their thousands, they died. And Kellory saw and knew it not.

In the very midst of the town of tents rose the black pavilion of the warlord, Prince Mnar. He it was who, in earlier years, had slaughtered the tribe of Kellory like beasts; it had been at the command of jesting Mnar that they had let one young boy live, after holding his right hand, his sword-hand, in the fire until it could never hold a sword-hilt to wield against them.

That child had lived and grown to become Kellory the Warlock.

He jested no more, did Mnar.

He came bursting from his tent, where he had busied himself by taking his pleasure of very young girls captured from Khev, to stare about him at the madness, the self-slaughter, the tumult. He could hardly believe his eyes as he looked upon chaos.

Kellory came up to him, and it was Mnar alone that Kellory permitted himself to see.

This Mnar was a tall man with heavy shoulders and a hard, cruel face, with shaven pate and eyes that glared like those of a wild beast. Half-naked was he, his swelling thews and dark flesh bare to the night-wind, save for scraps of leather and iron. In one great hand he clenched a heavy *ulthar* of black steel. He stared at Kellory, and for a moment they stood face to face, each looking into the other's soul.

It would have been difficult for Mnar to have recognized in the lean man in black the naked boy he had mutilated years before, hard for him to have remembered one victim among the thousands he had murdered. But he saw something in the green eyes of Kellory that made him flinch. He licked his lips, and turned his eyes away.

And then the Shadows were upon him.

Kellory strode on. Behind him a huddled thing cowered, screaming horribly, clustered about with shadow-shapes that whispered…whispered!

Prince Mnar ate of his own raw flesh, and died. But not quickly or easily.

# CHAPTER 8

## THE ENDING

The legion was there by dawn. As the sun-star rose up over the edges of the world, Almery looked upon a bewildering sight. The town of tents had caught afire and burned; now it was empty of all save corpses. Ten thousand of the Thungoda had perished or gone mad and fled like panic-driven beasts. These the revengeful knights of Khev hunted down and slew at their leisure. They had been at this pleasant task for half the night.

To where the High Prince sat wearily on the hilltop came Duke Almery to him with a thin girl with tired eyes, her bright hair matted with road-dust. The Prince swore feelingly, then crushed her to his heart. Few words were exchanged.

They looked towards the city. The man in black had gone there after spreading havoc and death through the Thungoda tents. Now was the city cleansed of its plunderers, and their corpses lay mingled with those of their victims.

And Kellory was gone.

None had seen him go. It was as if the night had taken him, as it took the Shadows, once their task was accomplished.

Kellory's task, too, was accomplished. And now he was gone. But where and how, no man could say.

"He told me once that when his task was done, life held nothing more for him," said Carthalla from cold lips in low tones.

"The Warlock devoted his life to the destruction of the Thungoda," said the Duke somberly. "Once that was done, to what lesser purpose could he turn his will? He lived for vengeance. Now that he has tasted it, life has no savor."

"Perhaps it is better this way," sighed the Prince. "I would have given him a dukedom; he would have been welcome at my court. But he would have been a grim guest, spreading fear about him, like a specter at a banquet. It is better this way, albeit I would have liked to thank him."

"He did not wish your gratitude," said Carthalla. "He cared little for other men. His only passion was vengeance. It was his life; his destiny…"

The Prince took her hand in his.

"Come; let us go down into the city, and see what Death has spared. Fear not for your Warlock. Whether he lives or dies, he has done his work in the world, and his memory will live on the lips of the troubadours of Khev for a thousand years."

They went down into the city, to see what the Lord of the Shadows had spared.

# PART 7

## THE GRAY ENCHANTER

# CHAPTER 1

## ON FIRE MOUNTAIN

For days the travelers had made their slow way through the mountains, but now at last they were in sight of their goal. At the edge of the chasm they dismounted from their shaggy ponies and stood to look upon Fire Mountain.

It was near to the hour of sunset, and the west was aflame. Against that fiery sky the peak soared, black and sheer, and flames danced upon its crest.

The guides and bearers licked their lips and glanced at one another. They could think of no reason why the woman had hired them to conduct her to this dreadful place, or why it was that she wished to go forward alone from this point. But they did not ask; cold silver can quiet curiosity.

Yothlymbris was the mountain's name, and it did not enjoy a favorable reputation. The men were glad they did not have to conduct their mistress thither, glad that from here they could turn back to their own village among the foothills.

Now they helped the woman to dismount. She was fair to look upon, even wrapped in her bulky furs, and a lock of her bright hair escaped from the hood of her garment to flutter upon the wind.

"You can cross the chasm at this point, lady," said their leader. "See, a great stone bridges the gap."

"Yes," said Carthalla of Khev.

She gave the man a bag of silver with which to pay the others, and waited while they removed her baggage from the pony's back. Then she bade them farewell, and stood watching as they filed back down the slope and vanished from view.

She turned to regard the mountain.

It was taller than its brethren, was Yothlymbris, steep and sheer. But there was a path to the crest from this side, her guides had told her.

Shouldering her bags, she crossed the stone and began the climb. They had told her that it would take an hour, perhaps two, for her to reach the crest, where the wall of fire danced. And she began the final journey without delay or hesitation, for she did not want to make the ascent in the dark. When she reached the top, she knew, she would find a bridge of iron which spanned the moat of fire, at whose center she would find the black castle.

She climbed.

* * * *

It had been three months and more since the Thungoda had been destroyed upon the plain before the gates of Grand Khev. For three months she had rested, regaining her strength after the grueling adventures and privations she had suffered. And for three months she had striven to forget the man by whose side she had endured them.

But she discovered that she was no longer the same woman who had ridden forth from Khev many months before only to fall captive to the Thungoda and be rescued by the Warlock. Garden parties, balls, fetes and feasts no longer diverted her, nor did the frivolous gallantries of laughing young courtiers and nobles. The adventures through which she had passed had made such idle pleasures seem empty and boring, after the excitement she had experienced.

And she could not forget the grim, bleak man who had shared those excitements with her.

Very different was he from any man she had ever known, a dark and somber, brooding man, hard and silent and cold. There was a maturity about him, a sense of purpose, which made other men seem vain and weak and foolish by comparison.

She wondered what he thought of her, and if he even thought of her at all. For in all the time they had spent together, he had never touched her, never sought to win her love: he seemed hardly to be even aware that she was a woman, young, fair and very desirable.

She climbed.

# CHAPTER 2

## THE BLACK CASTLE

She crossed the moat of liquid fire by the iron bridge, although it was red-hot. She did as Kellory had done years before, when first he had come to this place as a boy: soaked her boots in water and run across before the hot iron could sear her feet.

The great gate stood open, a titanic slab of ancient black wood, ajar as it had been when Kellory had first seen it. But now no more did the Sigil of Kellory's mentor, Phazdaliom, glitter from the wood in dust of emeralds. Now it bore another sign, that of a gloved fist worked into the wood with powdered gray steel.

The Sigil of Kellory? It could only be he, and Carthalla felt thankfulness well up within her heart, for until this very moment she had not been sure the Warlock would have come here.

Entering, she found herself in a hall of stone columns. Here, all was cool and shadowy, after the fierce light and blistering heat she had endured on the bridge.

She traversed the arcade and entered a long avenue lined with strange statues, at which she peered timidly. Now she was in the open air again, with the inner castle before her, a bizarre structure thronged with minarets and turrets, cupolas and balustrades, which rose tier upon tier against the darkening sky where the first few stars wavered uncertainly.

The avenue, she saw with amazement, was strewn with crushed diamonds. They caught the dim starlight and threw it back in a crazy tangle of flickering rays, reflected from ten thousand facets. Trembling just a little, she ventured upon it, treading underfoot the wealth of emperors. The statues which stood to either side were a rank of steel warriors, resembling fantastic suits of armor. Stiff arms brandished pikes and axes, swords and scimitars, in frozen menace.

As had been the way with the outer gate, the portal of the inner castle stood open, almost contemptuously inviting the traveler to enter, as if the owner of the black castle was indifferent to danger.

Within, she wandered through suites and corridors and apartments decorated fantastically. There were statues of shimmering ice, which stood unmeltably, and flowering trees fashioned of noble metals and precious gems, and fountains of colored smoke which jetted from bowls of alabaster. The floors were strewn with the hides of mythical beasts, the walls hung with curious tapestries whose woven figures or foliage seemed to move when you looked at them, and lit by lamps filled with cold, unearthly fire.

She wandered from room to room until she began to weary of the marvels. She sought the inner parts of the castle, for nowhere in these empty rooms did she discern the slightest sign of life. After what seemed like hours, she reached a portal framed by two giants of purple stone which turned eyes of luminous yellow crystal to observe her as she approached. Carthalla shrank fearfully from that glaring gaze, but the carven figures neither moved nor spoke, so she crept between them and parted a curtain of black gauze sewn all over with minute rubies.

And found the man.

# CHAPTER 3

## REUNITED

The chamber was tiled with octagons of jade and lapis lazuli, and roofed with a dome of pearly glass. The walls were lined with wooden shelves upon the which stood rows and rows of huge volumes bound between plates of wood or carven ivory, or leather and the tanned hides of beasts. In the far wall, tall, peaked windows looked upon a garden dreaming in the light of three moons.

In a huge, throne-like chair of black wood sat a tall, lean man with a clean-shaven, dark face. He regarded her wordlessly from cold green eyes.

"You were a fool to come here," he said harshly.

"I didn't know where else to look for you but here," she said, "in your master's house."

"It is my house now," he said somberly, "for Phazdaliom, for all his wisdom, could not hold Time at bay forever. His centuries have claimed him at last. I laid him in his tomb."

Tears brimmed in her eyes but she fought to keep from crying. She fed her eyes with the sight of him. He was different, she saw: gone was the gaunt, weary man who had faced so many perils and wrought such wonders as had made his name a legend in the Seven Cities. Now the weariness had been erased by the months he had rested, and some of the hardness was gone from his face, with the satisfaction of his lust for vengeance against the Horde.

Then she noticed the manner in which he was dressed, and her eyes widened a trifle.

"What is it?" he demanded. She forced a shaky laugh.

"Nothing, really; it's just that I was so accustomed to seeing you in black leather…"

He glanced down at the long, loose robes of gray silk which clothed his lean body, and shrugged a little.

"My master wore emerald green, by which reason the people of the mountains called him the Green Enchanter. Now that I go robed in gray, for aught I know, they term me the Gray Enchanter. It matters little what name a man bears…"

"Why gray?"

"After what I worked before the gates of Khev, when I sang the Song from the wizard's Book, I did not think white was suitable," he said. His face was expressionless, but Carthalla almost laughed, for it was as near to a jest as any words she could remember from his lips. But there was a grimness underlying the words that chilled her. For she remembered how he had driven to madness and death the Thungoda in their savage thousands…

Kellory rose to his feet.

"I forget my courtesy," he said. "You have come for, and the road was wearisome. You must bathe, and rest; then we shall dine together and talk. Come."

* * * *

They dined at an oaken table drawn up before a roaring fireplace, carven of malachite in the likeness of snarling dragons, and Carthalla was impressed by the richness and the delicacy of the food, which was excellently prepared and wonderfully spiced, with rare sauces and wine of a superb vintage. Surely, the Warlock did not cook his own meals, and she had as yet seen no sign or token of servants. But she did not inquire: if the meal was made by magic, or had been whisked hither by invisible spirits bound to the Warlock's service, she would rather remain ignorant of the fact.

They talked little. After all, there was little to be said. They both knew why she had come here and what she wanted of him. They avoided the subject, and talked of trivial things, when they talked at all.

He escorted her into the moonlit garden and took a seat beside her on a bench of lustrous crystal, luminous as an enchanted diamond.

"Kellory…"

He looked at her and the words she was about to utter died unspoken. For his face was hard and cold, and his eyes were passionless.

"You should not have come," he said heavily. "I know what you want of me. It is something I do not have to give."

"Tell me that you are happier since we parted ways, and I will leave," she whispered.

Nothing changed in his eyes, but his voice was softer when he spoke.

"I cannot tell you that, for it would be a lie."

"Well, then," she sighed, and came into his arms and put her mouth against his own.

# CHAPTER 4

## A THOUSAND TOMORROWS

After they had loved in the great canopied bed, they lay naked together and rested. And said what was in their hearts.

Kellory was very honest with the woman. He knew, and she knew, that it was unlikely that they could find real happiness together, but neither had found happiness apart. The months since he had vanished from the streets of Khev had been an agony of loneliness for the Warlock, although he tried to deny it. Nor had they been any better for Carthalla.

"My life was built for one purpose," he said, "and with that purpose accomplished, I drift idly with the days. I sought forgetfulness in my studies, but the books of sorcery hold not for me now the charms that once they held. Nor do I take any pleasure in the Power I possess...it seems a futile thing, life."

"And—love?"

"I do not know that I can truly love," he said dully. "The softer emotions I forced from my heart when I devoted it to Vengeance. Vengeance was my god, and upon its altar I killed the feelings a man has for a woman. I do not know that I can ever change."

"Then what are we to do?" she asked brokenly.

He shook his head. Then, after a moment he spoke.

"There are a thousand tomorrows ahead of us, whether you leave or stay. Somewhere in those tomorrows I may discover that which I have given up. But I may make you miserable..."

She kissed him gently.

"We might as well be miserable together, then," she said, with the ancient wisdom of her sex, "for surely we shall be miserable apart."

Kellory said nothing. He did not believe that her warmth could thaw his heart, for the chill sheath of ice was iron-hard.

He did not think that loving her would make him forget, even for the moment, the horror he had worked upon the Thungoda with his Song.

And he did not know if he could love her at all.

But it was worth trying.